DEDICATION

If you are reading this, I dedicate this book to you.
Without readers, a book is just words on paper. Thank
you for being a part of it.

A NEW DAWN

Book 3 in the Allison's Secret Series

D Stalter

CONTENTS

ACKNOWLEDGMENTS

The completion of this series would not have been possible without the encouragement and assistance of many people. Friends and relatives (especially Bruce) who shared their support and understanding are especially appreciated. A special thanks to Randileigh Kennedy and Denise Trout who gave their time to read and edit the manuscript.

Allison

"You are absolutely crazy if you think going to Rockford is a good idea." Allison felt the now familiar wave of anxiety overtake her. She struggled to breathe. The muscles in her shoulders tightened. She stood with Riley and Will at the counter that divided the kitchen from the living room. Behind her was the kitchen, the appliances now dusty.

They'd been unused for months since the power went out. The back door, with the large window looked over the yard and the path to the barn.

Across from the back door were the basement stairs which led to the living quarters of the security detail. Her dog, Bella lay on the kitchen rug.

She fought to gain control. "Every report we've heard says that Rockford was totally destroyed.

Even Chicago fared better." She slammed her palm on the counter. Her eyes flashed. "I can't forbid you, but I can beg you. Please don't go." Her eyes filled with tears. "Please. I can't bear to lose someone else."

Will looked at the floor before raising his eyes to meet hers. "I understand. I really do, but Riley and I have to make the trip. With luck, we'll only be gone a day – two at the most."

Allison looked at Riley, her eyes growing hard, before turning back to Will. "I need you here. Riley can go. Let him."

Riley glanced at Will, then turned and walked through the kitchen to the back door. Allison watched him step outside before turning to close the door behind him. His eyes met hers. He gave a slight nod and then closed the door behind himself.

Will waited until he heard the back door click.

"Listen, Allison," he said softly. "I understand that you don't like Riley. I don't know why, but that's your business. The only thing I want to say is that you need to ease up. Riley is not your enemy. He's been here helping you since the beginning. He's my best friend and whatever it is that you think he's done, it has to be based on a wrong assumption."

Allison sighed. "I'm sorry. The first time I saw him, I had a weird feeling. Every time I've seen him since, I have the same weird feeling. I get a knot in the bottom of my stomach. A sense of doom. And, to be honest, my sixth sense has never steered me wrong."

"Trust me. It's steering you wrong now."

Allison avoided looking at him. "I can't help it," she whispered.

Will reached out and took her hand. "Allison," he said softly. "Riley is a good man. He's helped build this community and works his butt off to make it safe. Whatever it is you are feeling, you have to set it aside. With James gone, we need men like Riley."

She nodded. "I know. Please go get him."

"No. You go get him. You have to reach out to him. Please fix this now."

She dipped her head, then turned and walked to the door. She hesitated before turning the knob and stepping out on the porch.

Riley stood at the well, his back to the house.

She watched him inspect the rope next to the well before clearing her voice and calling out, "Riley, will you come back inside, please."

He spun at the sound of her voice, his mouth hanging open.

She turned and went back in the house. She stood next to Will looking down at her hands. Her left thumb dug at the cuticle of her right thumb. The back door shut and the sound of Riley's footsteps approached.

She took a deep breath and looked up. "Thank you," she said. Her eyes darted to Will before coming back to Riley.

"Look," she started. "I want to apologize for being rude. I can't explain. I have no idea why I feel this way." She stopped and closed her eyes for a minute. "Okay, anyway I just wanted to apologize and tell you that I'll try harder to be nice to you. You've truly done nothing to make me dislike you. Can we start over?" She extended her hand.

Riley blinked, then reached out to shake her hand.

As their hands met, an audible snap filled the room.

They drew back their hands in unison. Eyes wide.

Will stood with his mouth open looking back and forth between them. "What the hell was that?"

Allison shook her head. "It must be the dry air. I'm sorry, Riley." She rubbed her hands together and looked at the floor.

Riley said nothing. He simply stared at his hand.

Will finally broke the awkward silence. "We'll be leaving late this morning. We'll need food for four days. I'm hoping to be back by tomorrow evening, but I don't know how long it will take us to get around Rockford on foot."

Allison nodded, the conviction she'd displayed a few moments ago against the idea now gone. "How are you getting to Rockford?" Her voice trembled.

"Don has loaned us his old Jeep. He's already got it loaded with sleeping bags and other supplies. I told him that we'd bring our own food, but I suspect we'll find that loaded in as well. I just want to make sure we have what we need to get in and out as quickly as possible."

"You're not planning on driving into the city?"

"No, we'll stash the Jeep south of the airport. Don says that the FEMA guys have taken over the airport so we'll go on foot from there."

"Have you got any radios to stay in touch?"

"No, but Don has the location of a couple of HAM operators he knows. If we need to get ahold of you, we'll find one of them."

Will looked at Allison before continuing. "Look," he said. "We are going to Rockford today. We didn't come here to ask permission. We came out of respect to tell you when we were leaving and when to expect us back. The security detail can handle anything that might come up."

The back door slammed shut. Megan strode into the room. She came nose to nose with Will. The smell of wood smoke was heavy on her clothes. "I just heard you guys are going to Rockford. I'm coming with."

"No, you're not." Allison and Will spoke at the same time.

"Yes, I am. My sister lives there. I need to go see if I can find her. Look," she said turning to Riley. "I'm on the security team. You guys know I can handle myself. I won't be in the way and I can provide backup for you guys. I just need to know that my sister is okay. I'm sick of worrying about her and her kids. I'm coming."

Allison backed up. "I can't let you. We can't just let the whole security team take off. We need you here."

"We've got enough guys to keep this place safe – and anyway, we haven't had any trouble for a while. You'll be fine for a few days."

Riley had been quiet, holding his right hand in his left. He looked up. "She can come."

Will spun around. "What? They need her here. We'll be just fine. We don't need her. They do."

He turned back to Megan. "Just tell us where your sister lived and we'll try to check on her for you."

"I'm coming with you," she said softly.

Will looked at Riley and then at Megan. Both gazed back at him. He shrugged. "Where did your sister live?"

"She wasn't in Rockford, she was on the west edge of the city, just north of Highway 20. A few blocks off of Meridian Road."

Riley leaned back against the counter. "Out by Anna Page Forest Preserve?" he asked.

"Yes, a few miles south."

"That's about five miles from my bar," Riley said.

"Yes, but it's on the opposite side of the river from where we will be." Will leaned across the counter and picked up a pen and paper. "Your bar is here, next to the river." He drew a river and placed an X near the middle of the paper.

"My place is here." He drew another X. "But, what if we can't get across the river? She wants to go clear over here." He drew a third X.

Riley pushed off from where he was leaning on the counter. He held out his hand for the pen. Will sighed before tossing it to him.

"We are coming in from the south." Riley drew a line up the paper. "I say that we pass right by your place and get to my place first. We can clean out my stores and haul them back to your house. We wouldn't want to risk any of the bridges by my place. The Jefferson Street, State Street and Walnut Street bridges are in the highest crime areas of town. We'd be going out of our way to go north to the Whitman Street bridge, so let's go to my place, haul out stuff back to yours and then use either the Harrison Ave bridge or we could scope out the bridge there on Fifteenth Ave as we pass. That used to be a pretty rough area so it might not be an option.

"But, then we can just follow Springfield Ave. out to Megan's sister's house."

Will massaged his temple. "I guess that would work."

He turned back to Megan. "Are you absolutely sure? I guarantee that it will be dangerous. We are going to get shot at. We might get ambushed. We can't concentrate on keeping you safe while we are trying to keep ourselves safe."

"I can help you. I don't need your protection." She smiled. "You know I can help."

"Go get your backpack," Riley said. "And make sure you bring a sleeping bag."

Megan grinned. "Thank you!" She spun and rushed out the back door. Riley pushed himself off the counter and followed.

Will placed his hand on Allison's shoulder. "We'll be back in a couple days. I promise."

She looked at the floor and nodded, refusing to watch him leave.

Riley Rockford

Four and five story buildings with jagged glass doors swinging in the breeze greeted the trio as they silently made their way through an industrial area just east of the river. A feral dog showed its teeth, then slunk off behind a pile of cars that sat where they had died. The setting sun glinted off the remaining glass in empty windows.

Dirt and ash piled against the buildings like black snowdrifts after a winter storm. Will stopped the group.

"Find something to cover your mouth and nose. We don't know what is blowing around in this air we are breathing." He pulled a handkerchief from a hip pocket and tied it around his head before moving off.

Riley spun at the sound of crunching glass. Megan paused mid-step and cringed.

"Sorry," she winced.

Riley nodded and continued following Will.

The streets and sidewalks were fairly clear of vehicles. The dirt and ash drifts against the buildings seemed undisturbed except for two spots. In front of doors to a couple of structures, the drifts had been shoveled, like snow clearing a path into the building.

These spots they navigated cautiously, quietly observing each one before moving past.

In the last block, before the industrial area gave way to houses with back yards and trees, Will stopped. They were just a few feet from the corner of the building. His hand came up.

Riley immediately took a knee, straining to see and hear what had Will's attention. He watched Megan do the same behind him. Her rifle was pointing up, but positioned in such a way that she could instantly bring it into shooting position, just like he'd taught her.

Riley heard a soft moan. He leaned forward, cocking his head to hear better. There! A whimper. Will turned to look back at him. A grin crept onto his face.

Riley furrowed his brows and pursed his lips. Then it came to him. He heard the soft sigh and a low whisper, "John, I love you so much."

He felt his neck relax just a little.

A deep voice broke the silence. "What the hell are you kids doing?"

A shriek. Rustling. A young girl's voice. "Daddy! Turn your back so I can get my clothes on."

The man continued. "Listen, kids. I know you're young and in love, but John is supposed to be on the roof doing look-out duty. What if someone was sneaking up here while you were doing that? You could get us all killed."

"I'm sorry, Mr. Strader. I'm so sorry. I came down to check on a dog, Liz was here and… well… things just kinda happened."

Will slowly stood. He looked back at Riley who shook his head. Will handed his rifle to Riley. Riley frantically shook his head, but took the weapon.

Will stepped to the corner of the building, held his hands away from his sides, and said, "Excuse me."

"Who the hell are you?" It was the older man.

"My name is William Mead. You can put the gun down. I'm not a threat."

"Then what are you? What do you want?"

Will still hadn't moved his hands away from his sides. "My friends and I simply want to pass through. We aren't looking for trouble. In fact, we'd prefer to avoid it."

"Kids," the man said. "Get back inside. John, you get your butt up there where you are supposed to be and Liz…" He paused. "Just go to your room. We need to talk later."

Riley and Megan listened to sounds of movement before Will lowered his hands.

"Okay, where are your friends?" The man demanded.

Will motioned for Riley and Megan who stood and stepped up to stand next to him. "This is my friend, Riley, and our friend, Megan."

"Where are you going?"

Riley spoke up. "Just a couple blocks from here. I used to own a bar down by the river. We're just here to pick up a few things."

"What bar?"

"Riley's."

"Yeah, I used to stop there once in a while when I got off work." He paused. "You said your name is Riley?"

"It is."

"I'm gonna shine my flashlight on you for a second."

Riley squinted when the bright light hit his eyes and then moved down to his shoulders before being switched off.

"Yep. You could be that same guy. Your bar is cleaned out. Nuthin' left in there."

"It's not the booze I want. I have personal items. Pictures and mementos. Why did you shine your light on my shoulders?"

The man didn't answer for a moment and then finally said, "Just making sure you weren't one of those JP guys." He opened his mouth to continue, then closed it and looked behind him. "Well, good luck, then." He stepped forward, offering his hand for a shake. Will was closest to him and took an involuntary step back.

The man chuckled. "I'm sorry. I forget that we all smell like garlic. It's our cook. She demands that we all eat garlic every day. Garlic and who knows what other crappy herbs she's adding to our food. All I know is that whatever it is, it works. Ain't none of us been sick. We stink like garlic, but we don't smell each other. Guess we're used to the odor."

"We've got one of those herbalist ladies too. She certainly knows how to use herbs."

The man nodded. "Yeah, our Bell knows what she

is doing."

"Bell?" Will asked. "My mom used to be best friends with a Bell McDonald. That Bell grew herbs. I can remember whenever I'd get a cold or something, Bell would send over tea."

"You know our Bell? Want to say 'hi' to her?"

"Nah, she wouldn't even remember me. This was twenty years ago. My mother's been gone for fifteen. Bell probably wouldn't even remember my name."

"By the way," the man said, reaching out again. "My name is Dan Stader." This time Will took the offered hand.

"Hey," Will said. "If it wouldn't be too much trouble, can we ask if it would be safe to come back through here in a couple hours?"

Strader grunted. "I'll relieve John on the roof in about an hour. When you come back, stop on that corner over there and whistle. I'll let you pass."

"Thanks, man. It's sad what our world has become. You guys have everything you need?"

"We do okay. We got holed up in here in the first few days. Most of us worked here. We went home and brought our families back and I'm not proud to say that we cleaned out a couple of stores to get what we needed to get through the winter. We're working on plans to move out to the country when it gets a little warmer. Find an empty farm, raise vegetables and try to find some livestock."

"Excellent idea," Will said. "Think that's the only way any of us will survive."

He turned to Riley and Megan. "You guys ready?"

Riley stretched his hand to the man. "Good luck, friend. I got a couple hiding places at the bar. If I find any booze, I'll bring a couple and drop them here. If there's more than I can carry, I'll drop a note here and tell you where to find them."

A huge grin spread across the man's face. "Good luck to you guys, too."

The door behind Strader opened. "Daddy, that Jersey guy is on the radio. He wants to know what's going on here."

Strader rolled his eyes. "Damn those nosey bastards. They got night vision goggles. They keep a pretty close watch on what's going on around here. If you take off now, they'll follow you. Come inside and wait for a bit. They get bored easy. They'll be gone in a while."

Will looked at Riley who shrugged and picked up his backpack before indicating to Megan to follow.

Megan's Sister

They stepped in to what had once been the offices of a successful manufacturing plant. The smell of garlic overwhelmed them. Megan scrunched her nose and breathed through her mouth, but her eyes still watered.

"Yeah," Strader said. "I know. Garlic. You get used to it." He turned towards an office. "I need to go answer Jersey or he'll send some boys over to check things out."

"Who is this Jersey?" Will asked.

"The Jersey guys control the city on the other side of the bridge. In one way, that helps us out because ain't nobody coming across that bridge except them. And we got a truce agreement."

"A truce agreement?"

"Yeah. In the beginning, we lost some guys to them and they lost some to us. But then, one day, Jersey's ten-year-old daughter got sick. Really sick. Bell offered to take a look at her so we met them on this side of the bridge. Bell came back and mixed up some medicine to give to the girl. She got better really fast."

He looked out the window. "Since then," he continued, "They've asked for medicine a few times. We always give it to them. Now we talk on the radio and make sure everything is good. Occasionally we need to cross the bridge to take someone over to the National Guard place."

"Wait!" Riley held up his hand. "They let you cross the bridge?"

"Yeah, as long as we ask first. Jersey's an asshole, but he mostly just wants to keep his group safe."

"Think he'd let us cross the bridge? Megan here needs to go check on her sister out by Anna Page."

"I can ask." Strader picked the walkie-talkie off the table. "What's up, Jersey?"

"You got company over there?" The voice crackled over the radio. "Everything okay?"

"Yeah, everything's fine. Just an old friend."

"Who's that?"

Strader looked at Will, who shrugged. "Remember the bar down the street, there by the bridge? Riley's?"

A chuckle came over the radio. "Yeah, that was the first place we cleaned out. Got some damn fine booze from there."

"Uhm, well, yeah. Riley is here."

"Tell him he ain't getting his booze back. I pissed it out a long time ago."

Riley held out his hand. After a short hesitation, Strader handed the radio to him. Riley pressed the button and said, "I'm glad you enjoyed the booze. If it hadn't been you, it would have been someone else. I didn't expect it to still be there."

"Well, yeah. That's true."

Riley pressed the button again. "I wonder if I can ask a favor of you."

"What kind of favor?"

"My two friends and I need to make a trip out to Anna Page Preserve. Think we could come across the bridge and head out there? We'll probably only be out there a couple hours or less. Then we need to head back here."

There was silence. Finally, the radio crackled again. "Put Strader on."

Riley handed the radio to Strader who brought it to his face. "It's me."

"Yeah, I'll let them pass as long as you come with

them. We don't want any trouble."

Strader raised his eyebrows at Riley who nodded. "Yeah," Strader said into the radio. "We'll take my Camaro. We should be coming across within the hour."

"Ten-four, good buddy."

Strader rolled his eyes. "I hate that guy," he said to the group.

As they turned to leave the office, Will stopped. He glanced at Riley and nodded his head toward the door. Riley took a look and his hand tightened on his weapon. The outer office contained at least ten people, all looking into the office they occupied.

Strader looked at them, then at the group outside the office. "Okay, guys, give these guys some room. They don't know you. You're making them nervous."

"Well, we don't know them either," someone said.

"Yes, you do." Strader stepped in front of Will and Riley and out of the office. "Come on, move back. You guys should know this by now."

The crowd backed up and Riley followed Strader out of the room.

"Hey, I do know you," a voice came from the back. "Didn't you run that bar down the street?"

Riley nodded. "I did."

"Well, the booze is gone."

"I heard. I figured it would be."

"Well, what are you doing here?"

"Just passing through."

"To where?"

Strader held his hand up. "Crosby, you're always full of questions. Do me a favor, will ya? Go get the Camaro and bring it out front. I'm gonna give these guys a ride. Oh! And stop and have Bell come up here."

"Sure thing." The man separated from the group and headed towards the interior of the building.

"Hey, Strader," Riley leaned around Megan to ask, "who are the JP guys?"

"They're from the government," A man in front muttered. "The president sent them to build his new army."

"He did not," another man protested. "They're fakes. Causing nothing but trouble. They are."

Strader held up his hand and looked at Riley. "We aren't sure who they are really. They say that the president sent them. They want us to join their army. If you refuse, they start shooting. I doubt they're from the government. But I have no idea what their real agenda is. We just try to stay under their radar."

A thin woman with gray hair walked briskly into the room. "You wanted me?" She pushed her wire framed glasses up.

"Yes, Bell. I thought you might like to see an old friend. Come here, Will."

Will pushed past Riley and Megan and stopped next to Strader.

"Hmm," Bell leaned forward, squinting. "Face looks familiar. Did you say 'Will'?"

Her mouth formed an "O" when recognition hit her. "Will Mead! Oh, my! The last time I saw you was at your mother's service. What? Almost fifteen years ago?"

"Yes, ma'am."

She took a step forward and wrapped her arms around him. "I'm so happy that you made it through this. What a terrible thing! You look wonderful!"

"As do you, Mrs. McDonald." He hugged her back, smiling down at the top of her head.

The throaty sound of a powerful car caused them all to look out the front windows as a bright yellow Camaro with underbody neon yellow lights pulled up to the curb.

"Seriously?" Will raised his eyebrows and looked at Strader.

"Trust me, this identifies me. When they see this coming, they know it's me."

"But what about the people further past this Jersey's territory?"

"Well, I'm positive Jersey has - or will - let them know we are coming through and to let us through. He's a jackass, but if he says he has your back, he does. If he ever looks at you and says 'You're dead' - you better run like hell."

He turned to the group and said, "We're running out to Anna Page Preserve. Probably back in about an hour. I'm taking one of the walkie-talkies. Call me if you need to."

They followed Strader outside and got in the car. When they got to the far side of the bridge, a man stepped out of the shadows to stand in the middle of the road. He was a well-built African-American.

Strader stopped the car and he approached from the driver's side. He carried a pink camouflage AR.

Strader rolled down the window. Jersey leaned down and peered into the car until his eyes settled on Riley. "Yep! I recognize you. Sorry about the booze, but if I hadn't taken it, someone else would have."

"I know. I don't hold any grudges. But I would like to know what happened to my bartender."

"That fat bastard?" Jersey laughed, showing even white teeth. "He holed up in there for three days. Had a shotgun. Anytime anyone would try to come to the door, he let loose. Wasn't nobody getting in there. Then, on the third morning, he just opened the front door. He had a backpack – probably full of your best booze – and the shotgun. He took off walking north. That's when we went in and took what was left. You know if we hadn't done it, someone else would have."

Riley sighed. "I know. And I promise there are no hard feelings. I probably would have done the same thing."

"Really?"

"No."

Jersey looked back at Strader. "If you go straight

out on State Street, my territory ends at Central Ave., but I got ahold of Wilcox. He controls out to Springfield Ave. He has no problem letting you pass. After that, you shouldn't have any trouble. Stop at each checkpoint and they'll recognize your car when you come back through. But stop anyway." He stepped back from the car and waved.

"What's with the pink camo weapon?" Riley asked Strader.

Strader grinned. "Dunno. Most of his shooters carry them. I never asked cuz, to tell the truth, I really don't want to get into a weapons discussion with him."

The checkpoint on the east side of Central Avenue waved them through, but the west side of the wide street was blocked by three cars. Strader coasted across the street, coming to a stop about ten feet from the barricade.

A woman stepped out. Dressed in drab fatigues and wearing laced up boots, she strode up to the car.

"Strader?" she demanded.

"Yes."

"Drive straight through. Don't slow down and don't even think about stopping. There will be a checkpoint at Springfield. You need to stop there so our guys can get a good look at your car or you won't be allowed back through on your way back." She eyed the muscle car with the neon underbody lights. "Although I don't think this thing will be hard to recognize. Just do it. It's the way we operate."

"Will do," Strader said. "I appreciate your hospitality."

"Mrrfff," she dismissed them as quickly as that, climbing in to the middle car and backing it out of their way to allow passage.

With Strader driving and Riley sitting shotgun, the drive down State Street was uneventful. Will leaned over to Megan in the back seat.

"How're you doing?" he asked softly.

She gave him a weak smile. "I just hope she's okay. And my nephews. The little one, Jared, is three. He's got asthma. I'm worried that all the smoke they said came from Rockford might have made him sick. I just hope they're all okay." Her voice trailed off.

Will reached over and took her hand. "I hope so too."

They both looked out the window as the car slowed for the final check point. On each side of the street, armed men watched them pass. When the car stopped, a man stepped up to the driver's window. He wore grungy jeans and a watch cap. His shotgun pointed at the ground.

"Strader?" he asked.

"Yep."

"How soon will you be coming back through?"

"Maybe an hour. Depends on what we find. We are looking for the family of the girl in the back seat."

The man leaned down and looked at Megan.

"Well, good luck. Please stop when you come back. We'll let you back through. It won't be hard to miss this car." He chuckled as he marched away to remove the barricade.

The car accelerated down State Street. Houses and buildings gave way to trees and open fields.

Megan looked at Will again. "I'm scared," she whispered.

"I would be too," he whispered back. "Is your sister married?"

"Yeah. Her husband is a machine repair guy. Paul goes to factories all over and fixes machines. Sometimes he's gone for a couple days. I think he travels as far as Minneapolis and I know he's been to Des Moines. But, even when he's home, he's not really home. He likes to run around with his buddies and go out to bars." She looked out the window, watching the landscape fly by.

"Paul's not a bad guy. I like him well enough. I just think my sister could have done better," she continued.

She leaned forward and tapped Strader on the shoulder. "Our turn is coming up. Go north on Meridian and then take the second right. It's not too far off State Street. Maybe a half mile."

They turned into a small neighborhood with well kept houses. There didn't appear to be any damage, but there also didn't appear to be any signs of life. Megan directed Strader to a modest single-story house with a fenced in back yard.

Riley and Strader exited and scanned the area. Nothing moved.

Will squeezed out of the back seat. He turned and offered his hand to Megan who took it with her own hand shaking so bad, Will had to squeeze tight to hold on.

"It's going to be okay," he said. "Come on. Which door does she use most often?"

"The side door by the garage." Megan's voice shook. She moved stiff-legged towards the side of the house. When she got to the side door, her hand fumbled with the doorknob. Will realized that it was a combination lock with numbers to push a code in to."

Megan offered a weak laugh. "I can't seem to punch the numbers in right."

"Maybe the solar flare took out the electronics," Riley offered.

"Oh, yeah. I forgot."

"Try knocking and calling her name."

Getting no answer, Will broke the glass out of the window. "I'll fix it before we leave," he murmured.

"Okay." Megan's whole body shook. Riley put his hand on the knob and opened the door while Will wrapped his arm around Megan and helped her into the house. Strader followed.

Megan

Riley moved quickly through the house. He didn't want Megan to be surprised by a scene she wasn't prepared for. Strader retrieved two lanterns from the trunk of his car and brought them in. He placed one in the living room.

But -- the house was completely empty. Dust coated every surface. There had not been anyone in this house for a long time.

Megan stood in the living room looking around. "Except for the dust, it looks exactly like the last time I saw it. I wonder where they went."

Strader had strolled into the kitchen with the second lantern. He now stepped into the living room and motioned for Riley.

"Look at the envelope on the table," he whispered when Riley walked in.

A 5X8 brown envelope lay in the center of the table. It, too, was covered in dust. Riley picked it up and blew the dust off. A note was written in black marker on the front of the envelope.

Megan, it read. We don't know you, but the letter

inside this envelope was written for you. We were passing by when we heard what sounded like a gunshot. We came to the door but no one answered our knocks. We decided to break in to make sure no one needed help. We found your sister (we think) in the kitchen with the letter inside this envelope. We buried your sister out back next to the two small graves. We are so sorry for your loss. It was signed, Tom, Adam and Jess. It was dated September 3rd.

"Shit!" Riley muttered. "How the hell do I tell her this?"

Strader shrugged.

Riley carried the envelope to the living room. He sat on the sofa and fingered the packet.

"Megan, come here," he said softly. Will looked at him and raised his eyebrows.

"What do you have?" Megan asked. She made no move towards him.

He patted the sofa. Dust floated in the air. "Come here. You need to see this."

"It's bad, isn't it?" Her eyes filled with tears.

Riley sat quietly, waiting.

Megan used the back of her hand to wipe her eyes.

She stepped to the sofa and lowered herself so she was sitting next to Riley. She raised her eyes to his. He saw fear and pleading. He handed her the envelope.

Without looking at the envelope she asked, "They aren't okay, are they?"

He shook his head. His own eyes filled with tears.

She took the envelope from him and bent her head, tilting the envelope so that the light from the lantern allowed her to read.

The envelope slipped from her fingers and hit the floor causing another puff of dust to gently float up before settling back on the wood. She did not pick it up to read the letter inside.

"Oh, God!" she wailed. "I should have been here." She jumped up and ran to the back door. Will followed on her heels.

Strader snatched the lantern from the kitchen table and followed them. The lantern wasn't needed. The light from the moon was enough to navigate the backyard. Strader hung back on the patio next to a square table with a glass top. Upturned chairs leaned against the vinyl siding of the house.

Riley joined him and they watched as Megan crumpled to her knees next to three lumps on the ground. Her sobs caused her shoulders to heave. Will stood silently next to her.

Strader leaned over and whispered in Riley's ear. "This is worse than I expected it to be. I really hoped we'd either find her alive or completely gone. This is sad. Really sad."

Riley could only nod. The lump in his throat threatened to explode and release what he felt in his heart.

He turned back to the house. "Come on," he said.

Once inside, Riley went to the first bedroom and pulled a pillow off the bed. Yanking the pillowcase free, he carried it to the living room.

From a shelf next to the TV, he pulled a photo album and carefully set it in the pillowcase. This was followed by the framed photos from another shelf. He glanced around the room before striding to the far wall and lifting a wedding photo off the wall. This he leaned against the coffee table. He set the brown envelope containing the letter on the coffee table.

The back door slammed shut. Will walked in with his arm around Megan. They stopped when they entered the living room. Megan lifted sad eyes to meet Riley's. "I'm sorry for that outburst," she said with a smile that didn't reach her eyes.

"Don't be sorry. It would have knocked me on my butt." He walked over and placed his arms around her shoulders. "Come here," he whispered.

He held her in his arms until she wiggled free. "Thanks," she said. "What are you doing in here?"

He held up the pillow case. "I'm collecting items that I think you might want to keep. I think I've got most of the stuff out of the living room, but you'll need to choose what you want from the bedrooms."

She turned without a word and walked down the narrow hall lined with framed photographs on the wall. She entered the first door on the right before turning around and asking, "Can I have the lantern? There's only one thing I want from in here."

Will brought the lantern and held it while she walked across the room to the dresser. She opened the second drawer and reached to the back, pulling out an ornate jewelry box. Without a word, she exited the room and gazed at the photos on the wall. She selected three before returning to the living room.

"Do I have room to take the quilt my grandmother made?"

"Of course," said Will. "Take anything you want.

We'll make room."

She strode back to the hall and opened a closet door. From the top shelf, she tugged a brightly colored quilt. She bent her head and held it to her nose, hugging it like it was a baby.

She handed the quilt to Riley as she passed. "A couple things from the kitchen," she said hoarsely.

Entering the kitchen, she opened a cupboard and pulled down a porcelain bowl. "My mother's," she said. From another cupboard, she added two coffee cups. "From when we were in college," she explained.

She stood in the middle of the kitchen turning in a circle, her eyes covering everything in the room. She shrugged. "I'm done."

They gathered the items, placing the brown envelope with the letter in the pillowcase. Riley considered offering it to her, but decided that if she wanted to read it now, in front of them, she would have. There would be plenty of time to read it later.

The trip through town was uneventful. Barricades were moved before they reached them. Jersey stood at the bridge. Strader pulled up and rolled his window down.

"Find what you were looking for?" Jersey asked

leaning down and placing his forearm on the car door.

"Not exactly what we wanted to find, but at least she can have some closure now."

Jersey stood straight and stepped back. "I'm really sorry to hear that. I truly am. Safe travels, my friend."

As they crossed the bridge, Riley looked over at Strader. "Can you stop at the bar?" he asked.

"Aw, man! It's gotta be after midnight by now. You sure you want to go through there now? Why don't you guys come on back with me. Spend the night in the factory and I'll bring you back to the bar in the morning."

Riley turned to look at Will.

"I don't know," Will offered. "Unless you want to spend the night at the bar and then catch up with these guys tomorrow. We'd probably be more comfortable at the factory. We got no reason not to trust these guys." He turned to Megan. "What do you think?"

"I'd just like to sleep. I can't believe how exhausted I am."

"Yeah." Riley looked at Strader. "We'll take you up

on that. Then, in the morning, I'll go get my mementos from the bar and if there's anything good left, I'll show your guys where it is. You can have it."

Strader turned right and slowly drove down the street next to the factory. When he got to the end, an overhead door slowly raised, two men lifting it and two men, further back, guarding.

"Leave your things in here if you want, we'll take this out in the morning."

Riley's Bar

They approached the bar from the back. The last time Riley and Will had stood at the back of the bar was the day of the solar flare when two young boys had taken Riley down in an attempt to steal his Harley.

The back door was closed. Its shiny white paint was marred by pry marks and the door jam was splintered. A slight tug opened the door.

Will stepped inside and moved toward the front of the bar. Riley stepped in behind him and held his palm out to Megan indicating she should stay watch at the door. The two men cleared the bar before collecting Megan and barricading the door from the inside.

"Upstairs," said Riley.

The dark staircase loomed before them. Will led the way, staying close to the back wall. At the top of the stairs, they again left Megan guarding the entrance and cleared the upstairs.

"It's clear," Riley told Megan. He bent over and pulled a soft bag from a nook in the wall. Reaching into the bag, he brought a handful of marbles out and laid them on the floor. He repeated this until the

A New Dawn

bag was empty and a four-foot square at the top of the stairs was covered in marbles.

"Poor man's security system," he grinned.

A long hallway ran the length of the building. Their feet scraped on the worn wooden floor. Riley ignored the first door, moving instead to the second door which opened to reveal a large single room apartment. The kitchen was on the far wall which would have been right above the bar downstairs. A sixty-inch TV was mounted on the wall near the door. On their right, an open door displayed a neat bathroom with a shower. Past that a small area was covered with an area rug. A double bed was centered on the rug.

Riley stepped to the far side of the bed. On the short wall closest to the bathroom, he reached under a shelf and pressed a button. After an audible click, the full-length mirror next to the dresser moved.

Riley walked to the mirror and swung it open and then stepped inside the hidden room. He reached up to the left and pulled a chain. The room lit up.

"Solar," he said to Megan's questioning look.

Megan stepped inside and whistled. "This is huge!" She paced to the far wall. "How big is it? It has to be 10 X 15, at least."

"You're close," he said with a smile. "It's 9 X 12."

"The stuff I want is in this corner. Help yourself to anything you see that you think you might want. Whatever's left, I'm giving to Strader."

They spent no more then fifteen minutes going through the contents of the room. Megan had assembled a small pile of knives and some books. Riley stepped over to a chest and pulled out a backpack. "Use this," he said.

They moved the marbles before going back down the stairs. Before stepping out the back door, Riley stepped behind the bar and pulled a screwdriver from a drawer. He opened a cabinet, removed three screws from the back of it and then pushed the cabinet out of the way revealing a door.

"Want to tell Strader to send his boys in?" He placed the screwdriver back in the drawer while Will moved to the back door.

Megan moved to the front of the bar. She used her hand to rub grime from the inside of the window. Pressing her face against the window, she peered down the empty street. Several cars covered with ash and dirt sat at the curb.

The back door slammed and she spun around – just as the front window exploded.

She flew back, landing on her butt between two tables, her mouth wide. Looking up at the window, she saw a hole in the glass exactly where her forehead had been two seconds earlier.

"Megan!" yelled Riley. "You okay?"

"I think so," she shouted back. "There's someone out there."

"No shit?" Will came around the side of the bar and crawled to Megan. He wrapped his hand under her shoulder and drug her backward until they reached a wide post. "Were you hit?" he asked.

"No, I don't think so. The bullet came in right where my head was a second ago. But the slamming door made me turn around and it missed me. Holy shit!" Her breath came in gasps.

"Stay behind this post," Will demanded. "It's made of steel. Shoot anything that comes in that front door. The front of the building is brick. Bullets can't get through that. The only way you can get hit is if they are close enough to the window to change the angle of the bullets. If they get that close, you'll have a better shot at them than they do at you. Just hunker down here and shoot anything that comes close to the building."

He bent down and looked in her eyes. "Can you do

that? Are you sure you're okay?"

"Yes, dammit! I'm fine. I can do it. Go get those bastards."

He moved away toward the back of the bar.

Riley motioned for one of Strader's guys to move up to the bar. The boy rushed across the open space and slid to a stop next to Riley. "Put yourself right here. Shoot from this side of the bar. I don't want you peeking around the other side and shooting from there. Megan has that covered and there will be someone further back covering it as well. Do you understand?"

The boy nodded, his eyes wide and his bottom lip clamped between his teeth.

"Hey," Riley barked. The kid looked up at him. "How much ammo do you have?"

Another shot broke through the window and buried itself in the back wall. The boy ducked.

"Hey, they can't get you from where they are. You are good here. The only way they could hit you would be to come across the street and stand directly in front of the bar. Megan would get them before they got a shot off. For now, the best they can do is use up ammo. Now, how many rounds do you have?"

"I think about forty rounds." He patted his pockets. "We're supposed to carry that much."

"Okay, don't shoot unless you can see them. Then just one shot at a time. You'll do fine. You're safe here. Come on, kid. Take a breath."

The boy sucked air like he was drowning.

Riley patted him on the back and moved toward the back of the bar where Will was talking to a kid wearing fingerless gloves. His stocking cap had slid back on his head revealing close cropped hair. His brows were furrowed. He stared at the front of the bar.

"Don't shoot our guys," Riley said as he progressed toward the stairway to the second floor. Will followed.

Another shot from outside came through the window and chips of wood exploded above their heads.

"Where's Strader?" Riley stood at the bottom of the stairs.

"He went out back with the other two kids. Said those bastards weren't gonna get his car."

Riley stepped to the back door and cracked it open. Strader was behind the dumpster. The two boys were out of sight.

"Is it Jersey?" Riley asked.

"No, it ain't him. He wouldn't do this. It's gotta be that gang from the north. They kill for fun. Assholes."

"We've got the front covered. Will and I are going upstairs for a better vantage point."

"Gotcha. Don't shoot me or the boys."

Riley cracked a grin before closing the door and motioning Will up the stairs. Several more shots came through the front window. Riley was proud that, so far, no shots had been fired from within the bar. It took self-control to hold your own fire when someone was firing at you.

Behind him Will started to sing, "Oh what a beautiful morning. Oh what a beautiful day. I got a wonderful feeling. I'm gonna fuckup somebody's day."

They reached the top of the stairs and followed the hallway to Riley's apartment. They made their way to the front windows. Riley chose the one on the north while Will slid next to the window on the south side.

Will looked at Riley who gave him a quick nod.

Rolling to his knees, Will eased his head over the bottom of the window to peer below.

"At least three shooters," Will said. "They're across the street. Two are hiding behind that truck. One is behind the car."

Riley eased himself to his knees and then raised his head to look over the sill. "There's another one in that doorway about twenty feet to the south of the truck."

As he spoke, three more shots rang out from across the street.

"I can take the one in the doorway," Riley said. "Do you have sight on the ones behind the truck?"

"Yeah, but not on the one behind the car."

"Wanna take those three out and then deal with that last one and any more we don't see?"

"Sounds like a plan to me. Tell me when you're ready."

"What the hell?" Will moved his head away from the window. "Sniper on the roof. Straight across from me."

Riley peeked around the corner of the window. "Pink AR."

"So, Jersey or one of his guys came to help. Who do you think he's helping? Them or us?"

Riley risked another look. As he watched the sniper on the opposite rooftop, the man raised his hand in a wave and grinned. It wasn't Jersey.

Riley held his hand up and then pointed to the doorway across the street. The man leaned over the edge of the roof and looked toward the doorway before raising his head and shrugging.

Riley held up his gun and pointed at the doorway again.

This time the man nodded.

Riley brought his gun to his shoulder. Three shots rang out from the opposite roof. Riley fired twice. The man in the doorway dropped. Three more shots rang out from the rooftop.

"Looks like they're all down," Will said.

"See any more?" Riley asked.

"Nothing moving down there at all. Come on, let's go check it out."

As they moved through the bar, Will told the kids to put their weapons away and go out back to tell Strader that the ones out front were taken care of.

Megan stood and followed the pair to the front door.

"Wait here," Will said. "Cover us if we need it."

"Okay." She moved away from the window to a spot that she could still see outside, but would not be in the line of fire.

Will slipped out the door. Riley followed. Will went left. Riley went right.

"Hey!" Riley called. "Pink AR coming around the northwest corner."

The man paused when he saw the men in front of the bar. He held his weapon in one hand and waved with the other. Riley waved back and the man continued toward them.

A door in the building across the street opened and another man exited. He too carried a pink AR. He crossed the street and held out his hand.

"Seth Thompson," he said.

"Will Mead."

"We've been following these JP guys for about an hour. Not sure what they were up to."

"JP guys?"

"Yeah. All four of them. They came from up by

Whitman. They saw them from across the river. Followed them as far as Jefferson Bridge. We crossed there and followed them here."

"Who are these guys?" Riley started across the street to see for himself. When he reached the first man, he kicked his weapon away before kneeling next to the skinny body. Grabbing his arm, he turned it to see a white patch basted on the shoulder. It looked to be a piece of bed sheet. In black marker, the letters J and P had been written.

Will approached with the Jersey guy. "That ain't no government patch."

The door to the bar opened and Strader hurried across the street. "Are we sure we got them all?" he asked.

"Yeah," Seth confirmed. "Jake and me been tracking them from Whitman. There was only four and we got them all. They got JP patches."

Seth turned back to Will. "Jersey said that you guys were just stopping by to pick up personal items from your bar. We'll take care of these four so you guys can get on your way."

"Thanks," Riley and Will spoke as one. Strader hung back to talk with Jersey's boys while Riley and Will returned to the bar. Megan still stood where they left her.

"All clear," Riley said. She breathed a long sigh. "That scared the shit out of me."

"I'll bet," Riley said. His eyebrows furrowed. "Are your sure you weren't hit?"

"No, I turned around when the back door slammed and that's when the bullet came through the window."

"What's all the blood from?" He came around the table and took her arm. "Oh, shit! I'll bet you scraped it when you hit the floor. We need to get that cleaned up."

He strode to the hidden room behind the cabinet and pulled a bottle of vodka off the shelf.

"Come here," he said. "Take off your shirt – you do have a t-shirt on, right?"

"Yeah, I'll be okay."

Riley was pouring the vodka over the wound when Strader came back in the bar. "What happened?"

"Think she got scraped when she went down. Who knows what kind of cooties are floating around in here. I'll get her cleaned up and we can do a better job when we get back home."

"Let's have Bell take a look. We've got water and she's a whiz with herbs."

"Great idea. Thanks. Let me gather my things up and show your boys where the goodies are hidden. If you want to give us a ride to the factory, we can have Bell clean this up and then we'll be out of your hair." He looked up from Megan's arm. "Or, we could walk to the factory if you want to stay with your boys."

"No, I'll give you a ride."

"Will," Riley called. "Would you take the boys upstairs and show them the room? There should be some broken-down boxes in the first room. Packing tape used to be on a shelf above the boxes. They can start packing."

While Will took the boys upstairs, Riley showed Strader the room behind the bar. Floor to ceiling shelves held beer, wine and spirits. Strader whistled. "This will keep my group happy for years! Thank you!"

Will

Bell took one look at Megan's elbow and quickly made a poultice from dried yarrow. She wrapped the arm in clean cloth, instructing them to remove the cloth as soon as they were in a cleaner environment.

She hugged Will goodbye, whispering that if he was ever in the area again, she would love to see him.

He grinned and said, "I'd make a special trip just to see you."

"Do that!" She patted him on the chest.

Strader watched as they packed their backpacks. "I'd be happy to take you to wherever you want to go," he said.

"Thanks, but it's not that far and I'd hate to draw any attention to ourselves."

"How far is it?"

"Not too far north of the airport."

"Well, I could drop you closer. Save you an hour or so of walking."

"Thanks." Will looked up from the backpack he'd

just finished buckling. "We appreciate every thing you've helped us with. If we get a chance to come back this way, I'd like to stop by, but for now, we've got to get moving." He held out his hand which Strader shook firmly.

"Where's the letter from my sister?" Megan asked.

"I put it inside the photo album." Riley stepped over, pulled the photo album out of her bag, and thumbed through it until he found the brown envelope.

"Thanks," she said, looking down.

"Do you want a chance to read it now?"

"No. I'm not ready yet."

It was almost noon when they arrived at the end of the block that led to Will's house. There were some signs of disturbance, but not total devastation as they had seen downtown. Broken windows decorated every house.

Will's house sat back from the street. It was a two-story, white plantation style home, with large posts in front of a wide porch. The second floor boasted a balcony that ran the width of the house. There were broken windows on both the ground floor and the second floor.

They approached the front door which opened to the touch. Will stepped in, followed by Riley and they quickly cleared the ground floor. The second floor was also empty.

The only other damage to the house was to the kitchen. Cupboard doors had been ripped off their hinges. Silverware and dishes were strewn across the floor. Will ignored the damage and went straight to the basement door. Riley started down the stairs behind him.

"Want me to stand guard here?" Megan asked.

"Please."

They climbed the stairs and were back in the kitchen less than ten minutes later. Both carried an additional backpack that were obviously stuffed as full as they could be.

"Do I want to know what's in them?" Megan asked.

"Nope."

"Are we going to wait until dark to head back to the Jeep so we don't have to sneak past the FEMA camp?"

"No. That would give them an advantage. I'm sure they've got night vision. Hell, everyone has night vision these days. We'll go as soon as we gear up.

Why?"

"Well, let me find a spot to go potty before we leave. Once I get loaded down, I'm not gonna want to unload until we get to the Jeep."

"Use the bathroom. It's still clean. First door down that hall across the living room."

Riley walked to the kitchen sink and peered out the window.

"I've been thinking," he said. "When we get back, I think I'm going to head down to Phil's and see if there's room for me there."

"What? Why?"

"I just think I'd be more comfortable down there." He turned away from the window and looked at Will.

"It's Allison, isn't it?"

"She's a witch."

"Come on, Dude. Give her a break. She lost her husband not too long ago. You'd be off if that had happened to you."

"I mean she's a witch." Riley closed his hands into fists, his nails cutting into the meaty part of his palms.

"Allison?" Will snorted.

"Keep your voice down!" Riley hissed. "Put it together. Herbs, medicines, electrocuting people she doesn't like."

Will chuckled. "You're not joking, are you?" He drew in his breath and then threw his head back and cackled.

"What did I miss?" Megan walked in to the kitchen running her fingers through her hair.

"Is he okay?" She jabbed her thumb toward Will who was still leaning on the counter. Tears ran down his face. Every time he glanced at Riley, he would snort and start giggling again.

Riley glared at him. "He's just an idiot. No brains in that big empty head."

Will continued to snort even as he bent to pick up the heaviest back pack.

"Come here," he said, motioning to Megan. "Let me help you with this." He held up the smallest pack and she turned around to allow him to slide it onto her back. Then he helped her adjust the straps before picking up a second pack.

Riley finished adjusting his backpack and picked up a second pack.

"I heard you guys say Allison's name while I was in the bathroom. What was the joke?" Megan asked as they walked out the door and turned south, toward the Jeep.

"Nothing." Riley shot a glare at Will who grinned.

Allison

Allison sat jotting notes at the table closest to the stove. A small smile tugged at the edges of her mouth. Her curly hair shone in the sunlight coming in through the window behind her. Writing notes and making lists always calmed her and today was no different.

Today she had her red notebooks spread out in front of her. The list she was working on was a rough estimate of what they needed to plant in the coming weeks to ensure enough food for next winter.

The canned items they'd been able to gather when the flare hit had helped them make it through the first winter. But now they would have to rely on themselves. Her red notebooks contained notes from past seasons.

She was trying to determine how many tomato plants they would need to feed forty people for a year. She had a list of things she needed to ask Jean and Mary for help on.

How many pounds of tomatoes did one plant typically yield?

How many pounds of tomatoes would they need to can enough for the winter to use in sauces?

How many canning jars did they need? Where were they going to find them?

She chewed on her pen and stared across the room at the children who were working on math problems. Fifteen-year-old Paul Wilcox was leading a group of younger children working on multiplication problems.

Eight-year-old Missy Funderburg and her twin sister, Sissy, argued at the table.

"No, it isn't," Missy said glaring at her sister.

"Yes, it is," her sister maintained.

"What's the right answer, Paul?" Missy challenged.

Paul gave her a small smile. "Your sister's right. The answer is eighty-one."

"Nine times nine is not eighty-one!" Missy's face became red and she pushed the whiteboard away. She stood up and stomped from the class.

"Allison," she demanded. "What is nine times nine?"

Allison smiled. "I'm afraid Paul and Sissy are right. The answer is eighty-one."

"Are you sure?"

"I am sure."

"Well, I hate multiplication and I'm not going to do it."

Allison looked down at her notes to hide her smile. "I completely understand, Missy. I'm struggling here too. Why don't we both call it a day and quit working with something that is stumping us. We can try again tomorrow when we are not so frustrated."

"Maybe I can help you," the young girl said as she sat down next to Allison. "I know that eight times eight is sixty-four."

"Very good!" Allison exclaimed. "But I'm afraid you can't help me because I need more information before I can start solving my problems. I'm going to see if Mary has some answers for me. If not, maybe Jean can help."

"Did someone call my name?" Mary stepped out of the store room. Her frizzy gray hair framed her plump face. A smile lit up her face.

Allison twirled the pen in her fingers. "I'm stumped," she said. "I'm trying to plan the garden but I haven't even gotten past tomatoes. I don't know how many pounds each plant gets. I don't know how many plants I need per person to provide sauces, ketchup, and everything else we need."

Mary came over and sat down. She looked at Allison's notes.

"I can help you with tomatoes, but the other vegetables we'll have to look up. Tomatoes you can depend on twenty pounds per plant."

She closed her eyes. "When I was a kid, I used to go to my grandma's house several times a year to help with the garden -especially at canning season. I can remember how, as we worked, she just talked and talked about what we were doing and why we were doing it. I don't know why I don't remember other vegetables, but I absolutely loved doing tomatoes with her. I remember her saying that five tomatoes plants per person would provide enough for the whole year."

Allison's eyes grew wide. "I'm figuring on forty people and each one needs five plants?"

Missy jumped up. "I know! That's two hundred plants!"

"Good job," Allison said. "This is all stuff that you'll want to know when you get older. Run back over there and keep learning."

Missy grinned before she skipped to the back of the room where the kids were still trying to solve multiplication problems.

Allison turned to Mary. "I miss James so much. I used to be able to worry out loud. He never had the answers for me, but he'd let me ramble until I figured out what to do."

"Aww, I'm sure you miss James, but I'm here for you. We can do this together."

"Okay, here I go." Allison smiled and then took a deep breath. "How do I plant two hundred tomatoes? And I know I need to get some started now. I asked Jack earlier how long until we could start using the greenhouse. He said that the greenhouse is better for extending the season. Not so great for starting plants. How am I going to get my plants started?"

"Well," Mary said. "My grandma used to start her plants in a cold frame. I've got a dozen or so old books in the basement in town that has tons of information that will help us. I do know that if we want to start in a cold frame, this is the time of year to do it."

"We need your books from town." Allison tapped her pen on the table.

"Yes, we do. I'll make sure that the next trip anyone makes in to town, they stop by my old house and get those books."

She pointed at Allison's notebooks. "Are you making to-do lists?"

"These red notebooks are all my gardening notes from past years. I haven't started my to-do list yet. But, I think I need to get started."

She pulled a green notebook from the bottom of the pile. "Green is for planning."

Her cheeks reddened. "James used to make fun of me for color coordinating all my notebooks. It used to really piss me off. But, I wish – just once – I'd look up and he'd be making fun of me again."

"I know, honey." Mary wrapped her arm around Allison and leaned her cheek on Allison's head.

Allison opened the notebook. At the top of the page she wrote, "HOW MANY PLANTS". On the first line, she wrote, "Tomatoes – Five plants per person = two hundred plants". Then she went down the page listing all the vegetables they would need to plant.

"As soon as we get your old books, we'll find out how many of each of those we need."

She turned the page and wrote, "THINGS TO DO," at the top of the page. Under that, she wrote "Cold frame?"

She looked up at Mary. "What else?"

"Build a root cellar," Mary said. "We were able to get through the first winter by using canned goods and stuff, but we are going to need a root cellar to get through the winters now."

"Yeah, I'd thought of that a while ago, but since I have no idea what I'm doing, it slipped my mind again."

"Well, between some of these guys we have here, and my old books, we'll do fine. One of those old books I was talking about was written in the early 1920's and the title is 'Farm Buildings'. I'm pretty sure there are some root cellar designs in there."

She closed her eyes again and her lips formed a smile. "I can remember my grandma's root cellar. She thought she was the luckiest woman in the world because Grandpa had run electricity out there. She had a light when she was inside – but she often mentioned that, when the weather turned bitterly cold, that one lightbulb could be left on and it provided just enough heat to keep the root cellar from freezing."

She made invisible designs with her fingers on the table while she searched her memory. "I remember there were two really thick doors to get into the root cellar. They were made out of some sort of heavy wood. They were about three feet apart. You had to open one door, take a step, and then open the second door. Grandma said that the airspace between them helped with insulation.

"When you walked in, the walls were lined with heavy shelves. The first thing on the right and on the left were all the vegetables we had canned. Past that was smoked meat. In the back was cheese Grandma had made. Grandma had some potted plants that she kept on the porch in the summer. In the winter, she would bring them to the root cellar and they survived until the next spring when she would put them back out."

A vehicle pulling into the driveway caused them to look out the window.

"Don's Jeep." said Allison. "It must be Will and Megan and Riley."

She moved to the door to meet the trio as they stepped into the barn. Riley was the first in, nearly colliding with her as she pulled the door open. His eyes widened and he stepped back allowing Will and Megan to enter before him.

Will had his arm wrapped around Megan. She cradled a photo album.

Allison reached out and touched Megan. "Did you find your sister?" she asked.

Megan's eyes filled with tears. She nodded.

"Oh no!" Allison understood. "Megan, I'm so sorry."

Megan whispered "Thanks" before slipping past Allison and mounting the stairs to her room.

Allison spun around to Will. "I need to go to her."

Will reached out and grasped Allison's wrist. "Leave her alone for now. She needs to be alone. Her sister left her a letter that she's been saving since late last night. She wants to be alone to read it."

"She shouldn't be alone." Allison tugged, but couldn't get free. She leaned toward Riley who backed up three steps before moving behind Will and slinking to the table where Mary sat.

"Let me go!" Allison snapped.

"Allison," Will spoke in a low voice. "It is a suicide letter."

All the fight went out of Allison. Her eyes grew wide.

At the table, Mary leaned back in her chair and

closed her eyes. "Lord, thank you for this group. Thank you for the knowledge and the ability you have blessed us with. Please give my friends the strength to move on. Shine your healing light on Megan. Help her find peace. Amen."

She opened her eyes and crossed herself.

"What happened?" She stood and walked to the stove where she poured herself a mug of tea. She looked at Riley and raised her eyebrow. He nodded. She brought another mug out and poured one for him.

"What did she find?" she asked.

"Someone had already buried her sister," Riley said. "Apparently Megan's two young nephews died and her sister committed suicide. Passers-by had heard the shot and found the sister. They buried her and preserved the letter with an explanation of what they'd found."

Mary clutched her hands together and shook her head.

"Megan is strong," he continued. "She'll work through this."

The sounds of sobbing filtered down from Megan's room. Mary rose and walked to the store room. She returned carrying several handkerchiefs and climbed the stairs.

Allison

Allison poured hot water over dried lavender and chamomile leaves in a teapot. While it steeped, she got the honey out and placed everything on a tray. She put three mugs next to the teapot.

She was halfway up the stairs when she paused, turned around, and came back down. She went into the store room and came back out carrying a bottle of brandy – which she added to the tray.

Mary sat next to Megan on the bed. Her arms were wrapped around Megan, her hand gently stroking Megan's hair.

They looked up when Allison tapped on the door and entered the room. Megan's face was swollen and wet with tears. She tried to smile but coughed and wailed.

Allison set the tray on the chair and settled on the open side of Megan. She brushed the hair from Megan's face. Megan lifted the paper she held in her hand and gave it to Allison.

Allison read, "Megan,

I'm so sorry. I can't do this.

Paul never made it home. I thought I could handle it

until he made it home. He was only supposed to be in Madison. He should have been able to drive home in an hour. I was able to fill the bathtub with water so we did have water for what I thought would probably be a day or two.

When the smoke from the fires came, it was horrible. I kept all the windows closed and stuffed rags wherever I could see smoke coming in from outside. But it was so thick. Sometimes I couldn't even see the driveway out the front window. I couldn't keep the smoke out of the house.

Jared couldn't breathe. I ran out of his medicine after about three days. I tried wetting rags and having him breathe through them, but it didn't help. His breathing got worse and worse. The night he died was horrible. It was raining, but I couldn't make Pauly sit with his dead brother in the house so I went out and dug the grave and buried him. I thought life couldn't get any worse.

But it did. Pauly and I didn't have any food left. I drained the water heater so we had a little more water, but poor Pauly cried all the time because he was hungry. I cried too because I was hungry and there was nothing I could do about it.

I kept remembering all the times you told me to make sure we had extra food in the house in case there was a snowstorm or something. I wish I'd just gone and done it instead of figuring I'd wait until winter to worry about snowstorms.

Yesterday I thought about taking Pauly and heading south to Princeton to see if we could find you. But I know Pauly never could have walked that far and I'm pretty sure I wouldn't make it out of Rockford. I'm just too weak.

Last night, when we went to bed, I decided that today would be the day we left the house. I didn't know what was out there, but it couldn't be any worse than starving, could it?

When I woke up this morning, Pauly was dead. He just died next to me in his sleep. I failed to keep my little boys safe. My heart is breaking. I'm so weak I didn't think I could dig his grave. But I did it.

Now I'm done. This is the only thing that I can do that gives me any control. I could choose to sit here until my heart stops beating. It will. I can't last another day. But I choose to make it quick. I only hope that I have enough strength left to hold the gun and pull the trigger.

I love you, my sister. You are the best sister I could ever have. If I am lucky enough to meet God, I am going to insist that I get to be your guardian angel.

Love,

Rita"

Allison felt a tear roll down her cheek.

I have no words, she thought. She wrapped Megan in her arms and rubbed her back.

"Allison!" Will shouted from below.

She gave Megan a final squeeze before rising and stepping out to the railing. She leaned over to see Will standing at the radio.

"Do you need something?" she asked with a sharpness to her voice that was rarely heard.

Will looked up. "Please come down and man the radio. Team One just called in that they saw some men hiding in the tree line. Then Team Three called in that they also saw movement. Riley ran to the house to get the other security members. I need to go out there. Riley will coordinate with the teams."

She was halfway down the stairs when they heard the first shot. She jumped the last three steps and rushed to the radio.

"Just keep everyone up to date," Will told Allison. "They should all be on the same channel now so they can all hear each other. You just let them know what is going on here and who is coming out. If they know the location of the attackers, make sure everyone knows. Riley will be back in a few minutes. And find out if that shot came from us or them. And, call Don on the radio."

He turned toward the door.

Megan and Mary had emerged from the room and were staring over the rail.

"Attackers?" Megan turned and headed for the top of the stairs.

"You are staying here." Will pointed at her.

"Oh no, I'm not."

"Yes, you are. If you want to help, get with Mary and get all the kids rounded up. Get everyone together. If they can handle a gun, make sure they have one and wait for instructions. If they can't handle a gun, keep them here and keep them safe." He didn't wait for an answer.

"Where are the kids?" Megan demanded as Mary was coming down the stairs.

"I'm pretty sure all the kids and most the adults who didn't have assigned duties are in the arena. I heard a couple of them talking about archery practice."

"Can you go bring them all in here and get a head count? I need to run out to the Jeep and get my gear."

She was just pulling her gear out of the Jeep when the door to the house opened and Riley stepped out followed by the security teams that were not on duty. She reached into her bag and pulled out her radio and earpiece. She held them up.

"Should I use these or does one of your guys need a set?" she asked Riley.

"Everybody good on radios?" He turned to the men behind him.

"I don't have an earpiece," one said.

Megan handed him hers and hurried back to the bunkhouse.

Mary had brought all the kids and parents into the bunkhouse. They huddled at the back of the room, wide eyes seeking reassurance. Mary was counting heads.

"We're missing Jaden and Paul," she said.

"Does anyone know where they are?" Allison looked up from the radio.

Sasha Wolff squirmed in her chair.

"Do you know where they are?" Megan demanded.

Sasha looked at the floor. "I'm not supposed to tell."

Mary looked at Megan and held her hand up. "Sweetie, it's important," she said, her voice soothing. "We need to find them and bring them here where it's safe."

"They went fishing." Sasha fingered her hair. "I wasn't supposed to tell."

"Do you know where they went fishing?" Megan's impatience caused her voice to rise.

Sasha shook her head. "No, but sometimes they fish down by James's grave."

Megan looked at Allison. "I'll go find them."

She met Riley at the door.

"Where are you going?" he asked.

"Jaden and Paul went fishing. I'm going to find them."

"Wait a minute. I'll come with you." He strode across the room and stopped at the radio, making sure to stay as far away from Allison as possible.

"The shot that was fired came from us. Team Three saw movement in the woods and reacted," she said.

He pressed the "Talk" button.

"Base to Will."

"Go ahead base," Will replied.

"I've sent three guys to meet with Team One, another three guys to meet with Team Three. I've got two more guys here at the bunkhouse. The shot that was fired came from Team Three."

"Thanks."

Riley pressed the button again. "One more thing. Jaden and Paul went fishing. Megan and I are heading to the river to get them."

"Ten-four."

"Arm the women," he said to Allison as he turned and joined Megan.

Allison stared at the radio. She hadn't heard back from Don. She keyed the radio again. "Allison to Don."

The radio remained silent.

She tried again. No answer. Tears streamed down her face. She sank into the chair and rubbed her eyes.

The radio squelched and then Don's wife's voice

came through. "Allison?"

Allison snatched the mic up and pressed the button. "Jean," she said. "Heads up. We've got something going on. Teams One and Three both have movement. Team One is positive that it saw men in the woods. Team Three reports movement in their sector."

"Yes, we've also seen movement. We heard a gunshot as well."

"That was Team Three. Someone just got nervous."

"We're good here for now. I'll stay by the radio."

"Please let your guys know that we've sent extra security out."

"I will. Thanks."

Riley

Riley scanned the yard around the barn. He pointed at the tree line behind the house. "I'm going to go over the hill here and straight down," he told Megan. "You move to the drive that goes down to the meadow and creek. Stay near the top. I just want you to watch for movement."

Riley moved off toward the tree line. A rustle of branches caused him to stop and assume a defensive position. A bush moved and Jaden darted out from behind it, followed closely by Paul. She spotted Riley and turned to rush in his direction.

"Riley!" Her voice was hoarse. She placed her hands on her knees, bending at the waist. She gasped for breath, finally gaining control of her breathing. "There's someone down there. We heard a gunshot."

Riley put his arm around her shoulders. "The gunshot was Team Three, but they did see movement. Where did you see someone? What did they look like?"

"We didn't see anyone. We heard the gunshot and then we heard someone moving around on the other side of the creek. We didn't wait around. We just took off."

Paul nodded. "Yeah, we left our fishing poles down there too."

Riley looked up to see Megan making her way back. He turned back to the kids. "You guys go on in. See if Allison needs any help keeping the kids entertained. Hurry, now. There are some concerned parents worried about you in there."

When Megan reached him, he squinted. "Are you absolutely sure that you are okay?" he asked.

"Yes, I'm fine. Let's go find some bad guys." She bounced on the balls of her feet.

"Actually, let's not go crashing into the woods when we don't know if it's bad guys or good guys moving around in there. I don't want to add to the confusion. I need to catch up with Will. I'd like you to watch the top of the hill and make sure no bad guys come."

"Okay. Will I get backup?"

"Just as soon as we can get someone back here."

"Go," Megan replied. "I'll be fine."

He stopped at the bunkhouse and stepped inside. At the back of the common room, the children were quietly working on schoolwork. They looked up, eyes wide, when the door opened.

Allison stood talking to Jaden. She spun to face Riley, her mouth open.

"Have you heard anything from Will?" he asked.

"Just a minute ago," she replied. "He's with Team One out near the highway."

"Please let him know I'm on my way."

"Will do."

He stopped at the door and zipped his jacket. Glancing over to the tree line, he saw Megan leaning against a tree, her back to him. He turned toward the highway and slid into the ditch.

He found Will hunkered down with Steve Mattern. Sliding in next to him, he asked, "What's up?"

Will sighed. "It's a standoff. They are sitting at the corner. They've got a pickup truck. I saw three guys in the back. The driver is standing on the other side of the truck. They know we are here. They know we know they are there."

"So, we just sit and wait? That's your plan?"

"Got a better one?"

Riley stood. "If they know we're here, let's just go see what they want."

Will turned to Mattern. "Bruce Willis, Sly Stallone and Arnold Schwarzenegger were hanging around and talking about a new action movie," he said. "Sly goes, 'I'm sick and tired of action movies. How's about we do a classical musical? I wanna play Mozart.' 'Okay', says Bruce, 'good idea. I'll play Beethoven.' 'Right!!' Arnold agrees. 'I'll be Bach."

Mattern was still chuckling when Will and Riley set off toward the truck parked at the highway.

"What do you think they are waiting for?" Riley asked. "They aren't hiding. It's broad daylight."

"Not sure." Will reached up and adjusted his earpiece. "I was thinking what I would be doing if I were them. The only thing I can come up with is that I'd be waiting for my teams to get into position."

They approached the truck, making eye contact with the man standing on the far side. He whispered something and the three men in the back of the truck slid some boxes against the cab.

"Hello, friends," the man said, stepping around the front of the vehicle. "My name is George Matthews.

I've been sent by the president to help survivors. If you give us just a couple minutes, we've got a few things to offer you."

"What kind of things?" Will wasn't taking the bait.

"I've got a couple smoked hams. We've got some beans. And we've got some homemade wine."

"Wine?"

"It's really good. We've got a group of women in Springfield that used to own a winery and they make the best wine. You'll love it."

He reached in the cab of the truck, and exposed an emblem with the letters JP. He pulled out a clipboard. "I just need to make a note of how many people you have and what their former occupations were."

Riley forced his face to stay calm. He glanced at Will and decided that Will had also seen the JP emblem on the man's shoulder.

"Why would you need that?" Will asked.

"The president needs to know what able-bodied citizens we have for when we start rebuilding."

Will looked from Riley to Matthews. "Do you mind if my friend and I have a private discussion?"

"Go ahead." He turned back to the men in the bed of the truck and directed them to load a box with ham and wine.

"The JP patch," Riley whispered. "How do we play this?"

"Their weak link is the skinny kid. Did you see how bad he was shaking? Let's go along with what they want for now. If we can get through this without dying, that would make me happy."

"How many people should we tell them we have?"

"Well, we have to assume they have radio contact with their other teams and know that we have other patrols out there, so let's go with a dozen. Just roll with this." He stepped back to the truck.

"We've got about a dozen people," Will said to Matthews. "We don't need your ham. You can save that for someone else. We don't drink so you can save the wine for someone else as well."

"Well, now," Matthews said with a smile. "I was hoping that we'd be able to sit down with you and get some paperwork done. The president wants a complete census. Really, this won't take long."

"How many are in your group?" Riley asked. "Is it just you four or are there more of you?"

"Nope. Just us."

"All right, come on back to the bunkhouse with us. Stay behind us in the truck. I don't want any of our guys to get trigger happy. You'll be better off if you let us escort you."

"Lead the way." Matthews grinned.

Will waited until Matthews was in the truck before he keyed his walkie talkie. "All teams stay where you are. We are bringing in this truck with four men. They say they are from the president. They claim they are alone and don't have any other teams. We know they are lying. All teams stay in position."

He turned and looked behind them at the truck, then he keyed his walkie talkie up again. "Allison, do you copy?"

"I'm here."

"Get the kids out of the common room. Have someone take them to the house. I'll want five men in the bunkhouse when we get there. Three should be hidden upstairs where they'll be in position to defend if they have to, but leave two guys in the common room as if they are taking a break. We've told these people that we have a dozen in our group so if they ask, that's the answer."

"Got it."

The truck stayed behind Riley and Will all the way to the bunk house. Matthews pulled in to the drive and backed up to the bunk house door.

Riley nudged Will and looked toward the skinny kid. Will's eyes followed his gaze. The kid wore torn jeans and a flannel shirt. The top two buttons were missing from the shirt leaving several inches of his chest revealed. Fresh thin wounds were visible on his neck. Below his neck, on his chest, wider wounds slashed across his upper body. Riley had seen wounds like that before, the day a fellow motorcycle rider had wrecked his bike and been tangled up in a barbed wire fence. The kid shivered, though it was not cold.

Matthews jumped out of the truck and approached the tailgate. "Grab those two boxes of ham and beans," he said pointing at the two nearest the back. "And grab a bottle of wine."

"I told you we didn't need your food." Will went around the back of the truck to stand next to Matthews.

"Ah, but you will love them. I promise." His smile was wide. He reached in and hefted the first box. "Grab the other box and the wine."

Allison opened the door to the bunk house. Her expression was questioning. "Can I help you gentlemen?"

"We're here to help you." Matthews gave her that wide grin. Riley was getting tired of seeing that smirk.

Matthews turned to his men. "Come on." He pointed at the skinny kid and his face hardened. "You stay with the truck."

The kid's face turned white and he simply nodded, looking at the ground.

"Put the boxes right there on that table," Matthews said when they entered the common room.

His eyes darted around the common room. They lingered for a moment on Rolly, who was seated in the far corner on the couches. A tattered magazine seemed to hold his attention. David Galen sat in a chair at the back of the room. He had a bucket of potatoes beside him and was peeling potatoes into a bucket between his legs.

Allison frowned. "Excuse me," she said, stepping between the men and the table. "I'm cooking here."

Matthews stopped and looked around the common room. He pointed at the next table. "Just set them there, boys."

He turned back to Allison. "You don't need to cook. I've got your meal right here. Ham and beans. It's already cooked and ready to eat. Just call your crew in."

Allison put her hands on her hips. "Listen, I don't know who you are, but we don't need your food. What I do need is to have my kitchen back. Now, you can take your boxes back to where you got them. I'm not cooking your food."

He raised his hands in front of his chest. "I'm so sorry. The president sent us. We are supposed to feed you and get a census report and explain to you what is going on and how you fit in to the president's plan for the future."

He pulled the lid off the box and reached inside to lift the lid off a crock. "Look, it's already cooked and hot. Just smell that!" He waved his hand over the crock sending the scent of ham drifting through the room.

"Just call your crew in and we can eat and then do business."

Will leaned in and spoke softly into Riley's ear. "He sure is anxious to get us to eat his food. Don't eat any of it."

"I've got an idea," Will said as he moved across to

the table Matthews stood at. "You sit down and eat. Then we'll talk."

Matthews eyes narrowed. "This food is for you. We ate just before we got here. We aren't hungry."

Will shook his head. "We aren't hungry either, so let's just finish our business here and you can leave."

Riley, still standing at the door, noticed the skinny man who had helped carry the boxes in start moving his hand slowly toward his hip.

Riley stepped forward and grabbed the man's arm. He thrust his pistol into the man's back. "Move your hand to the side."

The man complied and Riley reached down and slid a dirty 1911 out of the holster.

"Now you wait just one minute," Matthews spoke in a low voice. "The president himself sent us. What you are doing is considered assault on a government official. I'll let that pass if you just return his gun and put yours down."

Will stepped in front of Allison, his own weapon up, pointing at Matthews. "Turn yours over."

Matthews stared at him. The grin that had been plastered on his face changed to a frown. "You are making a mistake, my friend. I'll give you one more chance. I have the authority of the government. They won't let this go unpunished."

"Your gun." Will's eyes never left Matthews until he'd pulled his gun out and laid it on the table.

The third man, who was overweight, looked from Matthews to the skinny man, then raised his hands over his head.

"Put yours on the table as well," Will said.

After he had complied, David got up from his chair, dropping the potato he'd been peeling into the bucket. He walked to each stranger and patted them down. He recovered two more pistols, one from Matthews and one from the skinny man.

"Sit," Will said, indicating the table. All three men sat.

Riley brought plates to the table and spooned ham and beans onto each plate.

"Eat."

All three men began eating.

Riley brought three glasses to the table and poured wine.

"I don't drink." Matthews shook his head and held

his hand up in a 'stop' motion.

"Today you do," Will said.

The fat man was shaking so bad that he spilled his wine. Allison stepped forward and wiped it up while Riley poured a new glass.

"Drink," he said.

The three men picked up their glasses of wine and drank. The fat man's face twisted and he gagged.

"Drink it all." Riley stood behind the men.

Will addressed Matthews. "Do you really expect us to believe that President Arthur sent you to the middle of Illinois to feed a small group of people and take a census?"

Matthews snorted. "There ain't no President Arthur any more. President Phillips sent us."

"Who the hell is President Phillips?"

"President James Phillips. The President of Illinois."

Will looked at Riley who shrugged and looked at David.

David's eyebrows rose. "Wasn't James Phillips a congressman or something?"

Will's mouth opened, then closed. He looked at Riley and then walked around the table and sat down facing Matthews.

"Are you telling us that Congressman James Phillips made himself the President of Illinois?" He asked. "Tall, fat guy with a nose like Rudolph's?"

"Well, the government had gone to hell. Everyone in Springfield took off for home the day after the flare. The only government left in Springfield was Phillips and a couple aides. They weren't getting any help from Washington. When Phillips heard that President Arthur was dead and Washington was total chaos, he did what he needed to do. He's doing a great job putting things back in order."

Allison refilled the glasses with wine. Rolly had moved from the couch in the corner to stand with David.

"Drink it," Riley ordered.

"I'm not that thirsty," Matthews said, pushing the glass away.

"I said drink it." He moved around the table and stood next to Will's chair. "You aren't going to win this one, boys. Drink the drink you were going to have us drink."

The men drank.

The skinny man, his glass of wine still in his bony hand, was the first to nod off. His head bobbed a few times before he slumped over the table. Matthews turned his head to look at his teammate. His head started to bob. He slumped in his chair, chin to his chest.

The fat man grunted. Instead of lowering his head, he lifted it. The heavy lines between his brows deepened. He set his jaw and glared. "You gonna kill us?"

"Were you going to kill us?" Will asked.

"Probably not."

"Why would you have?"

The fat man shrugged. "If you fought, we'd have to. We were supposed to round you up and haul you to Springfield."

"Why?"

He shrugged again. "It's what Phillips wanted. He's the boss. And he isn't any president. I don't care what he says."

Will sighed. "You're gonna need another drink, aren't you?"

"If ya want me to go to sleep, I'll probably need a

couple more drinks. I'm a big guy. It takes a lot."
He shook his head. Greasy hair flopped on his
forehead. "But I'll talk. I won't fight you if you
want to leave me awake."

Will looked at Riley and raised his eyebrows.

"It'd be worth a shot," Riley said. "But, if he isn't
going to go to sleep, then I'd be more comfortable
tying him up."

The man placed his hands on the table in front of
him. "Do what ya gotta do."

"What's your name?" Will asked, tightening the
rope.

"Darren."

"Got a last name?"

"Yeah. Peters."

Will sat across from Peters. "Does the kid outside
have a gun?"

"Nah. Matthews didn't trust him enough."

"What's with the wounds on his chest?"

"The kid wasn't getting with the program. The last
straw was when he tried to escape. You either do
what Matthews tells you or you die. Matthews was

nice enough to give that kid a chance."

"Where'd the wounds come from?"

Peters sighed. He looked at the ceiling before lowering his gaze to the table. "Matthews is a dickhead. The kid refused to do what Matthews told him to do. He wanted to take his wife and go home. Normally Matthews would just shoot them and be done with it. But he liked the kid."

"What did he do?"

"Wrapped him in barbed wire and made him watch while Matthews raped his wife."

Allison gasped.

Will looked at David. "Go get the kid."

David started for the door. Rolly followed.

Peters sat back in his chair and yawned.

"What exactly was the drug you used in the wine?" Will demanded.

"I think it was the date-rape drug, Rohypnol. I don't know... Phillips has the women in Springfield make it."

"Women make this? To hurt other people?" Allison stared wide-eyed. She didn't blink.

"They don't have a choice," Peters said softly. "Phillips doesn't keep anyone around who doesn't do what he tells them to do."

"He kills them?" She was pacing back and forth in front of the table.

"He doesn't do it himself. He tells someone else to do it. Most the time Matthews is his go-to guy. Matthews likes it."

Allison's eyes filled with tears. "And this whack-job has declared himself in charge of Illinois?"

"He has. If you want to live, you do what he wants. If you do what he wants, the only thing that gets hurt is your self-esteem. It's kinda hard to feel good about yourself when you have to do what he wants."

"What was supposed to happen after we went to sleep?" Will leaned across the table. "How many more guys do you have out there?"

"There are two teams of three guys each. Before you went to sleep, we were supposed to get you to tell us how you called your security teams in. Then, we'd call them in and take them."

"Wouldn't have worked." Will sat back in his chair. He put the tips of his fingers together and moved them back and forth.

"Then we would have killed them." He shook his head and looked down at the table. "I'm sorry. Those aren't my rules. If I tried to disobey, I'd be dead."

"What were the plans for us?" Will pushed.

"Transport you to Springfield. Phillips has a process that he goes through. If you make it through the first inspection, you go into a group that he decides. If it works out, great. If not, he eliminates you."

"Why?" Allison asked.

"Because he needs complete control. He's building his army. He can't have the peasants sneakin up on him when he's not looking so he brings them in and turns the ones he can – kills the ones he can't. Like a vampire."

"Jesus Christ!" Riley spat.

"Haven't seen him," Peters muttered.

The door opened. David stepped in trailed by the kid from the truck. Rolly followed. The kid scanned the common room, his eyes finally settling on Allison. He nodded once.

He pointed at the skinny guy slumped over the table. "He dead?" he asked.

"Nah," Will drawled. "He just drank the stuff you guys were going to give us."

"Wasn't me." The kid's eyes grew round. "I didn't want to be with them. You need to kill them. If you don't, they'll come back and get you. And they'll bring friends. That's what they did to me." His eyes filled with tears.

"Sit down, kid," Peters said.

Riley pulled a chair out at the end of the table. The kid walked to it and slowly sat. He kept his full attention on the skinny man slumped at the table. "Did you get his knives?"

Will's eyebrows rose. He pushed the chair away from the table and stood to walk around to stand behind the skinny guy. Riley stepped over to help.

"He should stay asleep for at least four or five hours, but let's get them tied up anyway." He reached into the skinny man's pockets.

"No knives." He looked at the kid.

Peters grunted. "Look in his sleeves. Think he has arm sheaths."

Will lifted the man's bony arm and felt the cuff of his shirt. "Found one." He felt around some more. "There are three in each sleeve."

When he was done, six small knives lay on the table.

"Does he have a pen on him?" Peters asked.

"I don't see one."

"He has a knife that looks like a pen. Doesn't carry it every day, but I've seen it. He usually has a boot knife too. Better check that."

He did have a boot knife which was added to the pile of small throwing knives.

Allison

Will turned to Allison. "Get on the radio. Tell the security teams that we have at least six – maybe more men who are waiting to attack. Tell them to hold positions, but if they make contact, shoot to kill."

Allison hurried to the radio to make the call.

David and Rolly tied both Matthews and the skinny man to the chairs they had passed out in. Will nodded at the kid. "Tie him too."

The kid's eyes widened. "I'm not really with them."

"Sorry, kid. For a while at least, you're going to have to deal with it. I'd like to trust you, but I don't have time to keep an eye on you and I can't afford to make a mistake."

The kid held his hands in front of him and waited for David to tie him. "Please don't put me in the same place you put those guys."

Allison finished talking to the security teams and turned back to the table. She hadn't reached the table when the radio screeched.

"Team One to base."

Allison turned back and answered, "Go ahead."

"Allison, Jensen from FEMA is here. He says he has someone that wants to see you. He says you'll want to see her too."

"Who is it?"

"He says it's a surprise."

Allison looked at Will and raised her eyebrows. He shrugged. "Jensen is good. Send them in."

Allison relayed the message.

"Who do you think it could be?" she asked walking to the stove and placing the teapot on the burner.

"We'll find out in a minute."

Peters leaned forward. "You guys get along with FEMA?"

"Well, we aren't best friends, but they've helped us out a couple times. We haven't really had any problems with them. Why? Have you?"

"Well, not me personally, but before Phillips got ahold of me, I'd heard about some of the FEMA guys taking people away."

"Yeah. I think they did. But they left us alone. I think it depends on who the FEMA leader is and where they are."

The black SUV pulled into the driveway and Allison opened the door and stepped out. "Abby!" she screamed, seeing her sister tumble out of the vehicle.

She rushed to her sister and wrapped her in a hug. Tears ran down her face as she brushed her sister's hair from her cheeks. "How did you get here? Are you going to stay?"

"We delivered some documents to Jensen. We have to be back this afternoon but I needed to see you. I want you and James to meet my husband." She looked around. "Where's James?"

Allison stiffened. Abby drew back. "Allison?"

"James died a few months ago," she said softly.

"No!" Abby shook her head. "I'm so sorry, honey. What happened?"

"Let's go inside where it's warmer," Allison led her sister to the bunkhouse.

Riley met them at the door. He moved away as they passed him, then proceeded out the door to bring Jensen in.

Allison led her sister past the men at the table. Abby

turned to look at the four men who were tied up before following her sister to the back of the room where they settled into the couches.

Abby reached out and grasped Allison's hand. "What happened?"

"Do you remember Kim? She came through Davenport just after the flare. She said that she met you at the Army Reserve Center in Davenport."

Abby nodded. "I remember her. She said she was a friend of yours. Did she make it?"

"Yes," Allison said softly. "She made it. She didn't quite fit in. She didn't want to do any work. She shot James."

Abby sucked a deep breath. "No! I thought she was a little strange. But we were all a little strange in those first few days. I'm so sorry! I feel like it's my fault. I helped arrange a ride as far as Geneseo for her."

"It wasn't your fault. It wasn't anyone's fault except Kim's."

"What happened to that cute little girl? Her daughter. Was her name Kelly?"

"Yes, her name is Kelly. One of the families here adopted her. She's a sweet little girl."

Abby put her arm around Allison's shoulder and pulled her in. "I'm so sorry. Are you doing all right?"

Allison nodded. "There's too much to do to spend time mourning. In a way, that's a benefit. As time passes, I am actually able to think about what James would say or do, and it will bring a smile to my face. I'm too busy to be depressed."

She fingered the hem of her shirt. "I know if things were normal, I'd be moping around, driving myself insane with grief. But I stay busy from the time I wake up until the time my head hits the pillow. I miss him horribly. I find myself looking up when someone walks in the room, expecting it to be James. When I realize that it will never be James, I feel a little tug of grief, but I move on. Most of the time when I think of him now, I can smile. I remember how he used to make me feel. I accept that he will never be here again. And I feel his love in my heart. I can smile."

"Oh, honey, I'm so sorry!" Abby hugged Allison tight.

They both looked up as Riley entered with Jensen, followed by a tall young man wearing fatigues. He removed his cap revealing short brown hair. Allison recognized him immediately.

"Is his name, Josh?" she asked pulling back and smiling. "Kim told me you guys got married."

She stood and turned around to pull Abby up. "Introduce me to your husband."

He met them halfway with a grin on his face.

"Allison!" He stretched out his hands and took hers in both of his. "I know we've met at the gun store a few times before this all happened, but I've heard so much about you and James. I'm so happy to finally meet you properly."

Abby cleared her throat and looked at the floor.

"What's wrong, honey?"

"James passed away."

Josh's face fell. "Oh! I'm so sorry! Is there anything we can do?"

Allison felt a small smile tug at the corner of her lips. "Just be you. I'm so happy to see Abby find someone to complete her."

Will

"Allison," Will called from across the common room. "Can you come here? Peters here has some interesting things to share."

Peters leaned back in his chair. He yawned, his mouth open and ugly. "Damn! Those drugs really are potent. I never thought I'd be affected." He shook his head as though to clear a foggy brain.

"OK, like I was saying. We were supposed to make this one last run through Bureau and La Salle County getting a census of sorts, but mostly to bring back useful people. We are supposed to be back in Springfield by Saturday because Monday we are supposed to start this new phase."

The door slammed. Jensen strode in. "I've got a dozen men on the way to help deal with the guys in the woods. They should be here in fifteen minutes."

Allison turned away from Peters and asked Jensen, "Do you know who this group is?"

He nodded. "Oh, yeah. In fact, one of the reasons I was coming out here today was to warn you about them. They've been causing trouble all over the state. We had heard that they had a large group that traveled to the Wisconsin border and were working their way downstate taking prisoners and leaving dead all the way."

He leaned over, placing his knuckles on the table and dipping his face closer to Peters. "Where are your prisoners? Or did you kill them all?"

"They're safe," Peters muttered. "Listen. First, I want you to know that I was one of those prisoners last month. I had the choice to join them or stand in front of a firing squad. Learned real fast that if you join them, you still aren't free. They watch your every move. They'll kill you if they even think you might be planning something against them."

He lifted his bound hands and pointed at the skinny kid. "That kid has been through hell. This was his first trip with us. I could see it in his eyes that he was looking for a way to escape. Matthews was going to kill him."

The kid started shaking uncontrollably. He wrapped his arms around his chest giving himself a hug. His head swung back and forth. "No. No. No."

"Settle down, kid," Peters said. "I think you've finally got a way out without getting killed. Just help these guys. I don't think that they've got a chance in hell of stopping Phillips, but if we help them, their chances get a little better."

"Well," Will said softly. "We might have a chance. There's something I haven't told you all yet."

All heads swiveled toward him.

"Congressman James Phillips is a friend of mine."

Riley

"Shut up!" Riley shouted. He stepped forward, brushed against Allison and jumped back. He stalked around the table. "And when were you going to tell me this bit of news?"

"Geez, Riley. Settle down. I just figured it out a half hour ago. I've been trying to put all the pieces together."

He turned back to Peters. "Where are your prisoners and what exactly is Phillips planning?"

Peters sighed. "The prisoners are in two semis parked at an abandoned farm about five miles from here. Men are in one and women and kids in the other."

"They separate the families?"

"Yeah. It's easier to control the men that way."

The kid sitting across the table bent his head. Huge tears rolled down his face and dripped to his lap. Peters frowned. "Quentin there can tell you what happens to anyone who thinks they can get away with refusing to follow orders."

The kid shook his head.

"What'd they do?" Jensen asked.

"The kid here tried to sneak his wife out. Of course, they got caught. Matthews had one of the guys bring a roll of barbed wire in. Wrapped the kid up and then forced him to watch while Matthews raped his wife."

Jensen took a step back. His bushy eyebrows met in the middle and his jaw tightened. "And there are more of your men waiting out in the woods to come in here and do the same thing to these people?" The last words were almost a scream.

"Wait!" Peters said. "They aren't my men. I'm one of the people they kidnapped and forced to work with them. They have my wife."

"Where do they have her?"

"She's in the basement of a church building. She's working with the sewing crew. They make these patches." He turned slightly and dipped his chin toward the JP patch on his shoulder. "If I get out of line, she gets punished. If I escape, she gets punished."

He sighed. "Look, I'm afraid that even if you guys are able to stop Phillips, he'll get to the women and children and kill them before we can save them. I'll help you in any way that I can, but please help me get my wife back."

He dropped his head, chin to his chest. "We need to rescue all the families. Not just mine."

"I agree," Jensen replied. He pulled out a chair and sat across from Peters. "Now what exactly is Phillips planning for next week?"

"He's going to bomb all of the FEMA camps and offices."

"How the hell does he think he can do that? There are eight full camps and twenty offices."

"Like I said," Peters said, raising his head to look Jensen in the eye. "He's got a lot of people working in different areas. They are making the bombs whether they want to or not. Phillips's men keep a close eye on them. I was down in that building a week ago. There are cases and cases of bombs. Some are simple, but some are pretty sophisticated. They all are deadly. I know a few of them are considered dirty bombs."

"That makes absolutely no sense at all," Jensen scoffed. "A dirty bomb doesn't kill any more people than a regular bomb, any radiation wouldn't affect people immediately. A dirty bomb serves no purpose."

Peters shrugged. "The man is mad as a March

hatter. I think he just wants to be cool."

"What does he think he'll accomplish by bombing FEMA?"

"Well, that's just the first step that happens on Monday. Once FEMA is dealt with, he'll close the borders by blowing up every bridge on the west side of Illinois and post roving troops on the east and north boundaries."

The radio squelched. "Allison," the voice said. "Two car loads of FEMA guy are coming in. They are dressed for battle."

Jensen stood. "Wait for me. I'll get them moving to support your men."

Will followed him out the door.

When they returned, Jensen looked at Allison who sat next to her sister holding hands. "Any chance I could get a cup of coffee?"

"Of course! Abby? Josh? You guys want coffee?"

"I'd like tea if you have some," Abby said.

"I do." Allison moved to the stove.

Abby followed. "Let me help. I've so missed following you around the kitchen. James used to call us Frick and Frack." Her voice trailed off. "I'm sorry."

Allison smiled. "Don't be sorry, honey. We all miss James. I'd rather have his voice shouted than to have it whispered. He deserves to be remembered and talked about and laughed about. It helps keep his memories alive."

"We don't have much time," Abby said. "Josh has to be back in Davenport. A quick cup of tea and then we'll have to leave, but we will be back soon. I promise!"

They quickly assembled cups. Allison turned to the table. "Who all wants coffee or tea?"

Peters turned his head to look at Allison.

"Yes," she nodded. "I'll be happy to fix you coffee or tea."

"Coffee, please. One for the kid too."

When the coffee had been served, Will picked up the three gallon water jug. "I'll get this filled up. The extra security teams will be coming back as soon as they get those raiders rounded up. They might want some coffee." He ducked out the door.

When he returned, Jensen and Riley rose from their chairs. "We're going to leave one man here to watch the prisoners," Jensen said. "We're going to help round up the raiders. I want to get these guys behind bars before they wake up."

"Let me get this water on the stove to boil."

"I can do that." Allison moved to get up.

"No." Will put his hand on her shoulder and gently sat her back down. "I'll get this started. You sit and enjoy your sister."

Peters looked at Will. "Before you go, tie my hands behind my back like you've got theirs. I don't want them to think I got special treatment. For all they know, I went to sleep the same time they did. And," he nodded toward the kid, "don't put him in the same cell as any of the other guys. They'll kill him."

Jensen moved over and untied Peters hands. Peters moved them to his back and Jensen retied them. "Watch them," he said to the man standing guard.

"I will, sir."

Riley stood. Instead of moving directly to the door, he avoided passing Allison by going around the table. He felt his face grow hot when Will grinned.

"Kiss my ass," he hissed sliding past Will who held the door open.

"Bawk, bawk, bawk. Chicken."

Jensen zipped his coat before turning to Allison. "I almost forgot to tell you that you'll have a propane truck coming about 2:00 this afternoon. I took into consideration how many families you have here and put you down for two thousand gallons. I know you have two tanks and figured they were a thousand gallons each."

Allison's eyes grew wide. "That's fantastic! Thank you! But we only need about a thousand gallons. Our second tank is still at 50%. The first tank is at 20%." She held her hand up. "Wait! Do you think Don Schmidt could have my other thousand gallons? He's a part of this group too."

"Not a problem. I've got him down for six hundred gallons. Before I leave today, I'll write a voucher for the rest. You might want to let your guards know to look for propane delivery."

"I will."

"And I've got gas vouchers for you as well. I'll give them to you when we get back."

Jensen beamed and walked to the door.

"Hey, Jensen," Will called out. "What do chicken families do on Sunday afternoon?"

Jensen's eyebrows knitted together. "I don't know."

"They go on peck-niks."

Jensen smiled.

"Is chicken soup good for your health?" Will asked.

Jensen shrugged.

"Not if you're a chicken." Will chortled.

Riley rolled his eyes and walked in the direction he had left Megan earlier.

"Hey, Riley," Will called. "What do you call a scary chicken?"

Riley kept his head down and continued toward the tree line.

"A Poultrygeist." Will chuckled.

Riley

Riley slid next to Meagan who was leaning against a tree. "See anything?"

"One group of FEMA guys went down the hill past James's grave. The other went north towards Don's and then dropped down about there." She pointed to a spot about halfway between Allison's and Don's.

"I can't see what the second group is doing, but the first group is a little late to the party." She handed him the binoculars. "Look straight down there where the river makes the first bend."

He leaned against the tree and brought the binoculars to his eyes. "Our security team already has prisoners."

"Yeah, the funny thing is, there was no fighting. As soon as our team called out to them, they all laid down their guns and put their hands in the air."

"Sounds like they weren't that interested in a fight. Where are the FEMA guys?"

She touched his hand and guided the binoculars to the south. "Right in there somewhere."

"Yep. I see em. They are almost to our team with the bad guys." He watched through the binoculars while the FEMA guys approached the security team. The team handled the prisoners over to FEMA and waved before disappearing into the woods along the river.

Will and Jensen approached. "See anything, Chicken Little?" Will growled.

"Shut up, already!" Riley handed him the binoculars. "FEMA has the prisoners that Team Three captured. Team Three is heading back out and FEMA is bringing the prisoners in. We don't know where Team Two is. I'm going to head that way and see if I can spot them."

"Wait." Jensen held his hand up. "What's with all the chicken jokes?"

"Will's a jerk. There's nothing more to tell." Riley reached in his jacket pockets and pulled out his gloves.

Jensen looked at Will who shrugged. "Riley thinks Allison is a witch."

Jensen's eyebrows rose. "Seriously?"

"Think about it," Riley snapped. "She makes magical medicine with all those weird herbs. No matter what happens, she always seems to come out clean, happy and healthy. She acts like she's God's gift to the world. And, if she doesn't like you, stay away from her because she will zap you with a lightning bolt."

Jensen stared at Riley, his mouth open.

Megan giggled. The giggle morphed into a cackle. She stepped to Will and slapped him on the shoulder. "You need to let up." She chuckled.

"Why? He can take it. If he can't, he can't be my friend."

"Well, I kinda think she might be a witch too," Megan murmured.

Will bent his neck to look down at her. "Seriously?"

"Seriously. For the very same reasons that Riley gave – except she's never shocked me with her lightning bolt."

"That's because she likes you," Riley mumbled. "I'm going to see if I can help Team Two." He looked at Megan. "Want to come?"

"Nah. I'll go tell Allison what's going on and then wait for the other FEMA guys and let them know where you went."

Riley nodded. "Good idea."

He turned to Will and Jensen. "You guys coming?"

They set off to the north, following the tree line at the top of the steep hill. Riley paused every fifteen feet or so to lift the binoculars to his eyes and scan the river below. After the fourth stop, he said, "Got them. FEMA guys are herding them up a deer path. They should come out right about there." He pointed to a spot about fifty feet further.

They met the team at the top of the hill as they came out of the tree line. Several of the men were huffing from the strain of the steep climb.

"Any trouble?" Jensen asked.

"None. As soon as they saw us, they laid down their weapons and raised their hands. I left Stevie and Aiden down there to watch for any stragglers in case these guys were just a diversion."

"Good thinking," Jensen said. "I don't think it was a diversion. I think these guys might be looking for some help."

He studied the faces in front of him. "Any of you guys got anything you want to tell us?"

"They have our wives and kids." The man who spoke looked like he hadn't slept in a week. His hair hung out of his brown watch cap and was so greasy it glistened. He coughed, then turned and spit.

"How many of you are we dealing with?" Jensen

asked.

"Us three. Another three to the south and three guys with Matthews. Only one of them is not a prisoner. What'd you do with Matthews? He dead?"

"He's not dead. I need to be the one asking questions here. What was your plan?"

"They round people up, take their families and then make the men do their dirty work."

Jensen looked at Will. "You got your radio?"

Will pulled the radio out of his front pocket.

"Call Megan. Tell her to keep the other FEMA team away from the barn. Keep them down the hill until we have time to question these guys. Then we'll see if those guys give the same answers."

Will did as instructed before returning the radio to his pocket. He looked at the greasy haired man. "Who's the boss on this team?"

"Matthews."

"Who does he work for?"

"President Phillips."

"What's the end goal?"

"I don't know. They don't tell us a lot. But I heard that President Phillips wants to run FEMA out and cut off access. I think there might be a war going on and he wants to keep us safe." His voice trailed off.

"But that doesn't make a lot of sense," he continued. "He says that he wants to keep us safe in one breath, then in the next breath he's ordering someone killed. I sure don't know what's going on, but as long as they have our wives and kids locked up, we'll do what they tell us to do."

He looked from Will to Jensen. "Are you going to let us go?"

"Should we? What would you do if we did?"

The man shrugged. "Probably work down to Springfield and turn myself in. Tell them that we got ambushed and try to find a way to lay low until I can figure out how to rescue my family."

Jensen gestured toward the barn. "Take them to the bunk house and have them wait outside. Do not let them see Peters. If anyone asks, Peters was killed. Riley, Will and I are going to question the other prisoners."

They followed the tree line to the narrow road that led to the river. Megan waited with the other FEMA team. They had three prisoners sitting against a fallen tree.

Jensen strode to the three. "Who's your boss," he barked.

"Matthews." This was from a middle-aged man wearing a stocking cap and pea jacket.

"Who's his boss?" Jensen demanded.

"President Phillips."

"What was supposed to happen here."

The man looked at his feet.

"Answer my question."

The man raised his head. "We were supposed to capture everyone and take them to Springfield."

"Why?"

"Phillips needs troops."

"Troops for what?"

"I don't know. I heard there was a war."

"And what if these people put up a fight."

The man dropped his head again and muttered a response.

"I didn't hear you. What did you say?"

"I said that we were supposed to kill them. If you aren't with him, you're against him."

"You work for Phillips?"

"He has my daughter."

"What do you mean he has your daughter?"

"He has everyone's family. He keeps them locked up. If we don't do what he says, he'll kill them – or worse."

Jensen leaned closer. "What happens now?" He hissed in the man's face.

The man shrugged. "Hell if I know. You probably just got my daughter killed because if we don't bring prisoners to Phillips, someone will pay." His lips tightened. "I don't have a fucking clue what's gonna happen now."

Jensen looked at the leader of his men. "Tie their hands. Take them up the hill. We have seven more of them that we need to get in to town and put in cells. Get them locked up. Leave three men to guard them and the rest of you come back here. Somewhere there are a couple semis loaded with people they have captured. We need to go find them."

He drew the leader of his men aside. "There is a guy

in the bunkhouse that was with these guys. His name is Peters. You move on ahead and have Allison get him out of sight. Then, when these guys ask what happened to him, just tell them that you heard one guy died but don't know anything about it. I want him to stay here, but I don't want his buddies to know he's still alive."

"Gotcha." The man turned and quickly started up the hill.

Will

Riley, Will and Allison sat with Jensen at the long table in the common room. Peters sat at the end of the table. His hands had been untied and he rubbed his wrists.

"What exactly just happened?" Allison asked, setting the pot of coffee on the center of the table and placing sugar, milk and spoons next to the pot.

"I mean, I know that their plan was to capture us and take us to Springfield. But what I don't understand is how they thought they could get us to do what they wanted? Why wouldn't we just escape?"

"They've got it worked out pretty well," Will said. He pointed at Peters. "I think you should tell us exactly how Phillips operates."

Peters took a long breath. "I can tell you how he got me. They showed up at the farm we were at in the middle of the night. There were six of us on the farm. Three couples. We did okay. We weren't starving or anything and we had plans for putting in a big garden as soon as it warmed up. But, anyway, they got the draw on Snooky who was supposed to be standing guard. They got him so fast that he wasn't able to warn us."

He pointed at the coffee pot. "Can I have a cup?"

Will poured a cup and slid it over. "Milk? Sugar?"

"No thanks." He took a sip before setting the cup in front of him and wrapping his hands around it.

"They just snuck in the house," he continued. "We were all sound asleep and we woke up to three guys in each room. One guy ripped the wives out of bed, the other two grabbed the husbands. There really wasn't much of a fight. Nothing we could do."

He took a drink of his coffee and set the cup down carefully on the table. His hand shook. "One minute I was dreaming of a sandy beach. The next minute I had a gun shoved under my chin and an asshole telling me that if I moved, I was dead."

He closed his eyes. "They loaded us into trailers. The women and children in one trailer, the men in another. There were about thirty men in the trailer with me. They fed us watery soup and bread. It took four days to get to Springfield. They unloaded us into a huge warehouse. The men were still separated from the women and children, but we could see each other.

"That's the first time I saw Matthews. He stood in front of us and told us that the government had crumbled. The president was dead. Other states had gone to war. Our new president was Congressman Phillips. The new President Phillips was determined to keep us safe from invading forces. We were to become his newest soldiers."

Jensen snorted. "So you just followed blindly?"

Peters shook his head. "No. That's not what made me or any of the others follow him. What made us follow him was what happened next."

"Go on," Will said.

"Mathews looked at us and asked if anyone had any questions. One guy that had been in the trailer with me said, 'What happens if we don't want to be one of your soldiers?' Matthews pulled out his pistol and shot him between the eyes. Some lady screamed and Matthews had her dragged out of the group. He asked if she was the guy's wife. When she answered 'yes' he shot her too. Then he asked if there were any more questions. There weren't."

He shuddered. "They spent a week interviewing us and training us for being soldiers. During the interviews, they would ask questions and then tell us that as long as we followed orders, our families would be safe. The families were given jobs and a warm bed. That would continue as long as we did what we were told.

"There were interviews every morning and every night. Sometimes, after an interview, they would shoot a guy. Sometimes they got his wife and shot her too. Sometimes they let her live. I'm not sure what the decision-making process was, but I wasn't willing to test the boundaries."

"After a week, they let us see our families and spend some time with them. Then we were sent on our first raider mission. Again, if you didn't do exactly what the leader of the group told you to do, it was over for you. I just followed directions and tried to think of a way to get my family out of Springfield."

"I had a plan. In order for it to work, my wife had to escape while I was on the road. Whenever we returned from a mission, we were allowed to stay with our family. We were working on it and probably would have gone for it the next time I was sent out. Now I'll never know if it would have worked. Now I know that, as soon as Phillips finds out the group was captured, he'll kill my wife."

Jensen leaned forward, placing his elbows on the table. "What was your plan?"

"We hadn't decided the end game, but they take the women to their jobs every morning. They hang around and make sure that each person knows what they are doing that day and has the necessary supplies. Then they leave and just guard he building. But, at the end of the day, they just open the doors and lead the women back to the jail. They've got guards, but nobody seems to count or keep track of the women.

"The last time I was back, I was able to watch from a window. After they got the women back to the jail, they went back to the warehouse. They were in there for about an hour. After an hour, they turned off the lights and left. They had carts that they loaded into trucks and left. The building wasn't even guarded at night. I think they load up what was done during the day and close it up.

"We were working out a plan where, on the third day after I left, she would hide in the building instead of leaving with the other women. After the building had been cleared, she would sneak out and head south. She's already started going straight to her room every day so no one would miss her until supper time. She's even shown up late a couple times for supper so her absence wouldn't be suspicious right away."

He took a deep breath. "I would also disappear on the third day. It would be much easier for me. I would work my way back and we'd meet up somewhere south of Springfield."

"Where?"

"Hadn't worked that out yet. It would have to be close enough that she could make it in five or six hours. And we were thinking that it would be safer in a small town than in an abandoned farm house.

"There is a huge lake on the southeast side of Springfield so that would create problems either going around or crossing. But, to the southwest of Springfield there's a little town called Loami. I was leaning towards there. I was through there once. The town looks undamaged which is surprising considering the damage done while people were fleeing and rioting. But, it's off the beaten path and not on a major route. We didn't see any people there when we went through, but I'd bet there are some left. If there are, they aren't friends of Phillips and I bet they would help her."

Jensen leaned back in his chair. "All right, now tell us about the prisoners you have and who is guarding them."

"The trucks are at an abandoned farm a couple miles north and a little east of here. The farm is at the end of a dead-end road. There are six men in one truck and eight women and six kids in the other truck. Matthews left two guards. Both are die-hard Phillips fans. If we walk in without Matthews, they'll shoot."

"How many prisoners have you delivered to this

Phillips?" Allison demanded.

"About a hundred." Peters looked down at his hands. "But I've saved quite a few too."

"What do you mean you've saved a few?" she mocked.

"If I had a chance to let a few sneak out, I would. If I had a chance to warn them, I would. I didn't warn you because you were already on top of it from the minute we saw you. Most the time, I'd wait until Matthews and Sticky weren't looking and I'd try catching someone's eye and shake my head. It worked a couple times."

"But when it didn't work, you had no problem turning them over to that monster?"

She jumped as the back door banged open. Megan stepped in. She rubbed her hands together before picking up a clean coffee cup and pouring. When she turned to face the group, they were all staring at her.

"What?"

"Nothing," Allison said. "This guy was just telling us how he would turn families over to that Phillips."

"If I didn't do what they wanted, I would be dead. I wouldn't be able to warn any more people. If my wife and I could have escaped, we would have found a FEMA camp and would have told them what was going on."

"So you just went along with what they wanted and turned a hundred people over to him?"

Will stepped forward and put his hand on Allison's shoulder. "Allison, that's enough. I would have done the same thing."

Allison pulled back, her mouth opened and closed. "You wouldn't!" she insisted.

"I would," Will replied. "I would try to find a way to warn people, I would try to help them escape, and I would try to find a way to escape myself. It's actually the only way FEMA could have been warned and been able to stop what was happening. This guy couldn't stop it. He couldn't refuse to do it. They would have killed both him and his wife. So, let's stop blaming him and see how we can fix it."

Allison felt his hand squeeze her shoulder. She took a deep breath and relaxed. "Fine. You don't need me for this. I'm going to the house to see how the kids are doing."

"Wait!" Jensen stood and reached in his pocket. "I have gas ration books for you."

"Gas ration?"

"We are getting gas delivered to John's station in town. Each family gets a book with twenty stamps. Each stamp is for five gallons of gas. Each book is good for one month. I have ten books for you. At my last count, you had twelve families here, but this was all I could allocate right now. I'm hoping next month to have more."

Allison stared at the books he handed her. "So, we have propane being delivered this afternoon and we can buy gas now too?"

"We are starting to see the end of this. And we will be getting more shipments of other commodities in the weeks to come. That is if Phillips doesn't cut the state off from the supplies. We have to make sure he doesn't succeed."

"Thanks," Allison said. She took the booklets to the storeroom before exiting the bunkhouse.

Will

Jensen rubbed his nose. "Now, what are we going to do about this Phillips? We can't let him go on kidnapping people and building his army and we definitely can't let him cut Illinois off from the rest of the country. We're finally starting to rebuild."

"I know what to do." This from Will who leaned against the wall closest to the table. "I'm going to kill him."

"How do you plan on accomplishing that? The way it sounds, he's got quite a system that protects him."

"All I gotta do is meet with him. He'll be happy to let me get close."

Riley turned in his chair to face Will. "Tell me again how you two are friends? I've known you since boot camp. I've been to your family's gatherings. I've never seen or heard you talk of Phillips."

Will nodded slowly. "Didn't have a reason to talk about him. When I was in college, his brother was my roommate. James Phillips was a couple years older than us and had his own place. We used to hang out together. After college he tried to stay in contact. We did go out a few times, but I joined the service and he went in to politics. I'm sure that he'll let me get close."

"What makes you so sure?" Jensen had poured a cup of coffee and now held the pot toward Will who held his cup out for a refill.

"My last year of college, James Phillips was already out and working on political campaigns. His brother Bob and I were three months away from graduation. We were all three out one night. There was a drive-by shooting. Bob was killed. I was devastated – but not as devastated as James. We became really close over the next couple of months while we tracked down the guy that did the shooting."

"Did you find him?" Riley asked.

"Yeah." Will set the cup on the table and closed his eyes. "We found him. Now it's time to find James Phillips."

Peters grunted. "Did you kill him?"

Will narrowed his eyes. "This is about Phillips. I'm going down there to stop him from ripping this state apart. I'm going to need you to tell me how to get to him."

Peters raised his hands in the air. "Sorry! I'll help. You don't have to be so touchy."

"I'm going with you." Megan looked up from her cup.

"No, you're not." Will challenged.

"You aren't going alone."

"Yes, I am."

Riley shook his head. "No, you are not going alone. I agree that Megan isn't going, but I am."

"No. If I go in alone, I can get to Phillips. If you – or anyone – is with me, there is no way he'll let me close. If he allows just me in, then I'll have to worry about what's happening with you and I won't be able to concentrate on what I have to do."

"Which is?"

"Kill him."

Megan looked at Jensen. "You can sit there and listen to him talk about killing someone? You aren't even going to suggest that it's illegal to kill someone?"

"No, I'm not. This isn't the world we lived in last year. We are finally starting to see the light at the end of the tunnel. As long as Phillips is out there, we can't move forward. And, if he truly is planning on separating Illinois from the rest of the states, we will be moving backward instead of forward. If you think what he's done up to now is bad, wait until he gets rid of FEMA and cuts the state off from help. This is where I say something that I ever thought I'd say. 'Sometimes a man just needs killing.' I think Will can get the job done. I think we have to trust Will to get it done."

Megan shook her head. "He's not going alone."

"Yes, I am."

Jensen held up his hand. "I hear what you both are saying. I agree with Will that he has to do it alone. It's the only way to get close to Phillips. But I also agree with Riley and Megan that you shouldn't be completely alone. Here's what I think we can do."

He walked to the stove and poured another cup of coffee. "We found an old truck with a topper. In the back of the truck was a Yamaha. It's a 250cc trail bike. Apparently, whoever owned it was a competition rider for those road and trail races. I can't remember what they said they called them."

"Enduro," Will said.

"Yeah, that's it. Anyway, having a bike like that would make sure you can get around either on road or off road. You and Riley can go to Springfield. Before you get there, find a spot for Riley to hide out with the truck and you go on in with the bike. We can fit you with long range radios. You'll be going in alone but Riley will be there to back you up if needed."

"That would work," Will agreed.

"I'm going too," Megan said.

Will sighed. "There will be no discussion. You will stay here and help protect the community. Allison needs you here."

"I'm not letting you go without me." She crossed her arms over her chest and glared.

His eyes clouded. "I'm not putting you in any more danger."

Riley's eyes grew wide. "Shut the front door! You guys are sweet on each other!"

"Shut up, Riley," they said in unison.

"They are sweet on each other." He grinned at Jensen.

Jensen shook his head. "I don't know which one of you two is the biggest trouble maker. Let's get this figured out so you guys can head to Springfield. I think I'll send a couple of my guys to tail you. When I get back to town, I'll get ahold of the

Commander down there and see how they can help."

"I wouldn't do that," Peters said.

"Why?"

"Phillips has the same radio frequency. How do you think his guys were always able to stay ahead of you?"

"He can't know everything. We have protocols that ensure privacy."

"Hey." Peters held his hands up. "I've never seen the radios. I've only heard some of the guys talking about having heard what FEMA is doing on the radio."

Will shook his head. "I'd prefer you didn't send anything down there. I feel better doing this on my own."

"Well," Jensen said. "I will still send a couple of my guys to shadow you. I'll give you a map to the FEMA office down there and you can stop. I'll give you a letter to take."

"That won't work either," Peters said.

"Why not?"

"Phillips keeps a crew out by the FEMA office.

They report everything that comes and goes there. If they see these guys, Phillips will know."

Jensen sighed. "Let me think." He glared at Peters. "How far out from the FEMA office does Phillips post his men?"

"I don't know. I'm not exactly privy to what they do. I just overhear sometimes. I try eavesdropping every chance I get so I can learn things that can help me get my wife out. But, from what I've heard them say, it has to be fairly close because they use binoculars from a hilltop."

"Okay. If my guys leave you a ways back, and go in, it won't matter if Phillips sees them go in. They can't describe you if you aren't there. My guys can give the Commander a heads up and figure out where Riley can wait."

Will stood and walked to the stove. He poured another cup of coffee before he sat back down. "Actually, Riley and I are used to working alone. I'm not comfortable adding people we don't know into the mix. I want to be able to get in, get the job done, and get out. Riley and I have done this before. He knows his job. I know mine. Extra men would just get in the way."

Jensen scratched the top of his head. "I just can't get with that," he said. He turned back to Peters.

"What day did you say Phillips was going to launch his attack on FEMA and shut down the borders?"

"I heard that Monday was the day we were supposed to hit FEMA. I don't know if he's hitting the borders on the same day. I know he's got a lot of soldiers, but I don't know if he has enough to carry out everything in one day. For every prisoner like me, he has to have a soldier. But Monday is the day I heard we were supposed to be sent to blow up the FEMA camps and offices."

"That gives us five days," Jensen said to Will. "I'm going to send a couple guys down tonight. They can stop at the FEMA office in Peoria and share what we learned and then head to the Springfield office in the morning. They should be back by tomorrow afternoon. We will have more information then. Nothing will go over the radio. You sit tight until tomorrow afternoon. Okay?"

Will nodded. "I can do that. I've got some things to take care of anyway. It'll give me time to prepare."

"Great. I'll be back out here tomorrow afternoon and we'll get you on the road. My guys should be back any minute to go find those semis with prisoners."

He turned back to Peters. "Can you help us with the location of the semis?"

Peters shrugged. "North a couple miles, then east. It's a dead-end road. The road ends right at the driveway to a farm. Right off the road is a big corn crib. The semis are parked in there. The house is painted grey. It's a two-story with an open front porch that stretches across the whole front."

Jensen looked at Will. "Does that sound familiar?"

Will shook his head. "Not to me, but I'll bet either Allison or Don would know."

"How many men do they have guarding?" Jensen asked Peters.

"Three."

"Are any of those three prisoners like you?"

Peters shook his head. "Nope. They are all hard-core Phillips guys. You'll have to go in serious."

He placed his elbows on the table and leaned forward. "I can tell you that those guys have orders not to unlock either semi. They usually end up setting up a table and playing cards. There have been a couple of times that we walked in from a raid and they were all three sleeping. But then, sometimes all three are up walking around. So, it could be easy or you could have a fight on your hands."

Megan stood. "I'll go ask Allison if she knows the farm he just described. I'll be right back."

She returned with a plat book and a message from Allison that the property was easily accessible if one approached from the far side. It was only about a quarter mile through the woods from that side and their approach would be completely concealed.

"She said that there used to be a road that went through, but about thirty-five years ago a flash flood washed out a bridge over a little creek that runs through there. They never replaced the bridge so the road is a dead end on both sides now. You should be able to walk across the creek this time of year."

Megan poured the last cup of coffee. "Want me to start another pot?"

"Not for me, my guys will be here any minute." Jensen held his hand up.

Megan said, "Allison also said that as long as we were getting propane delivered, she'd like to run the generator and cook in the house tonight."

Will nodded. "That's a great idea. It'll be a little bit of a treat. Does she want help starting the generator?"

"I think she's got it."

Riley turned to Jensen. "You want us to come with you?"

"No. If you guys could keep Mr. Peters here until I get back, I'll pick him up and take him to the city jail later. I want to keep him away from the rest of the gang. I don't want them knowing that he's still alive – just in case they find a way to get word to Phillips."

"We can take care of Peters."

Jensen gathered his men outside and used the plat book to go over the plan. They'd been gone only a few minutes when the big LP truck rumbled down the road.

Every member of the group who was not on security detail lined up outside to watch the propane being pumped into the huge tanks.

"Do we get showers tonight?" Jaden asked Allison.

"I think that would be wonderful. Let's give the water heater a little while to heat up then we can start with the youngest and work our way to the oldest."

"Yay!" Jaden jumped up and down and clapped her hands. "Beth, you want to come with me and start gathering clean clothes for everyone?"

Beth turned to the barn. "I'll grab a couple boxes from the store room."

They almost skipped into the barn.

Mary turned to follow them. "I'll gather the food to take to the house for dinner. I'll need a couple healthy kids to help carry things."

"I'll come." A chorus of young voices made her smile.

"I'll go gather what dirty laundry we have," Lisa Grant said. "Want to help?" she asked Karen.

"Sure!"

"Do you need any help with anything?" Riley asked Allison.

She smiled. "Thanks. Actually, I've got a couple boxes of things in the basement I'd like brought up. I've got several chargers and a bunch of rechargeable batteries that I'd like to get charged up. I never worried about them before because we were conserving propane and didn't run the generator enough to keep things charged. Now, we can plan on using it enough that we can count on charging batteries. There are also some other things in those boxes I'd like help going through."

"I'll be happy to help." Riley smiled back. He

stepped away. "I want to go check on Will before I go in. He was going to try to see if that Peters guy could give him any intel on how to get close to Phillips."

"Hey!" she called.

He felt his shoulders stiffen. He paused and turned to face her.

"Give me about twenty minutes. I need to see if Lisa, Jaden or Mary need any help. I'll meet you in the house in about twenty minutes."

"Sure." He breathed a sigh of relief and turned back toward the barn. Why the hell had he just committed himself to being in close quarters with a witch?

A half hour later Allison and Riley sat across from each other at an old wooden table in the basement of the house. Each had a box in front of them and was sorting items. Bella lay next to Allison's chair. Her chin rested on her paws.

"I've got a solar battery charger here that will charge different size batteries. It looks like it will charge everything from AAA to D size batteries. Why haven't you been using this?" He held up the charger – still in the box.

Allison looked up, frowned, and then looked away.

"I don't remember even buying that. I thought everything I had required electricity to recharge batteries."

"Well," Riley brought out several more packages. "It looks like you may have purchased these rechargeable batteries at the same time. There are twelve each of AAA and AA. The package says they are good for 1.000 cycles. And right underneath them are two 8-packs of D-sized batteries. These say Energizer on them."

"Is there a receipt or anything? Because I seriously don't remember buying a solar charger."

Riley lifted the batteries and set them on the table. "No, that's everything in this box."

Allison slumped over the box she was sorting. "I must have picked them up and just forgot about it. Here, help me sort these into piles."

She scooped up a handful of Lifestraw water filters and handed them over the table. Riley reached out, but pulled his hand back before taking them.

"Give me a break," Allison snapped. "I'm not a witch. I'm not going to zap you."

Riley's mouth dropped. He felt his heart beat a little faster and his face grew warm.

Allison stared at him for a moment before her face grew red. "You really do think I'm a witch!"

"No, I don't," Riley stuttered before reaching out and snatching the drinking filters from her hand.

"Yes, you do."

"No, I don't. It's just..." His voice trailed off.

"Just what?"

"Well, you make medicine from herbs and you're always one step ahead of everything and then…" he paused.

"And then what?"

"You zapped me in the kitchen."

She threw back her head and laughed. "That was static electricity, you jerk. The house was dry. Don't forget, I got shocked as well. It wasn't pleasant for me either."

Riley sat back in his chair. He opened his mouth to speak, thought better of it and closed his mouth. He sighed before moving the empty box to the floor. "Which box do you want me to sort next?" he asked.

"I'll get it." She pushed back her chair, went to the shelves on the far wall and pulled another box off the shelf. Setting it in front of him, she lifted the lid. "These should be things like solar blankets and odds and ends. Last summer I planned on putting together bags for each of our vehicles. I was buying things to put into the bags and storing them together here until I had time to put the bags together. I just never got around to it."

"A get-home-bag," Riley said.

"Exactly. I was lucky I didn't need it that day because it wouldn't have done me any good sitting on a shelf in the basement."

"Weren't you home when it happened?"

Allison chuckled. "I was in Davenport buying ammo. Actually, when it hit, I had just started home. I was passing the Quad City Airport when I saw a flash of color to the north and then my Jeep died. Within the next few minutes, I watched a plane crash and I got chased by two men. I don't know if they wanted to talk or they wanted something worse, but I've never been so scared in my life – until I was almost home and I saw two motorcycle thugs a mile from my house sitting on the side of the road with guns."

"We weren't motorcycle thugs," Riley said softly.

"Well, I know that now, but I was so scared that

day. You could have been eighty-year-old ladies in wheelchairs and I would have been afraid of you." Her nose wrinkled and she giggled.

"Is that why you hate me so much?" Riley looked into her eyes.

She stared back at him before slowly nodding. "Probably. I've wondered myself why you make me so uncomfortable. The only reason I can think of is that the very first time I saw you almost threw me over the edge with the fear I was dealing with. You were standing next to that big bad Harley. You had a rifle in your hands and you were just staring at me."

She lowered her eyes. "And for the record, I never hated you. I was afraid of you. I didn't know why, but I was. I'm sorry for that. I'm sorry I treated you so horribly."

"And I'm sorry for everything too. I'm sorry that the solar flare happened. I'm sorry you had to see me sitting on a Harley adjusting my guns. I'm sorry you had the impossible task of building a community. I'm sorry about James." He paused and looked at the ceiling.

"I'm sorry I just mentioned James. You don't need more reminders of that horrible day."

Allison moved to the couch and sat. "It's okay," she said. "When he died, I thought my world ended. For the first couple of days, I didn't think that I would ever survive without him. But there was so much work to do. So many people depended on me. I just forced myself to go on. It surprised me how fast I was able to deal with him being gone. I think it's because I had so much to do. I know it's only been a couple of months, but I'm looking toward the future. I wish James were here, but I'm fine. I'm doing what he would want me to do. I'm living my life and helping others live theirs."

She looked up at him. "Does that make sense?"

"It makes perfect sense. You are one strong woman."

"I'm not a witch."

"I know."

"Prove it," she challenged.

"Prove it? How?"

"Come sit next to me and take my hand."

"Aw, come on." he pointed at the box. "We've got work to do."

"Chicken," she taunted.

He felt his jaw tense. "Have you been talking to Will?" he asked.

"No, why?"

"He was full of chicken jokes this morning."

"Oh!" She laughed. "I did hear him tell a couple of them. So, are you going to take my hand?"

Riley shook his head. "If it will help you move past this and get back to work, I'll hold your damn hand." He stood and walked to the couch. He sat on the end furthest from Allison and reached out his hand.

Allison grinned.

"What are you grinning about?" he asked drawing his hand back. "You are going to shock me, aren't you?"

She giggled. "I was just thinking that I wish I had drug my feet across the carpet before I sat down. That would have been a hoot."

Riley snorted. "That's just cruel." He reached his hand out again. She took it in hers. His eyes widened at the little jolt of electricity he felt in his fingertips.

"Well, crap!" Allison drew her hand away. "That

didn't quite go the way I planned."

She looked over at Riley who sat on the far end of the couch, his mouth open.

"Maybe it's you," she said. "Maybe you are the one shocking me. You ever thought about that?"

He stared at her, his mouth open, before shaking his head. "Let's get back to work. Tell me what you want me to do with the stuff in that box."

"What do you think? Should I still put a couple get-home-bags together or should I just take all this stuff up and put it in the storeroom to use as needed?"

"I think a couple go-bags could be useful. Like if someone needed to travel further than ten or fifteen miles, they could throw a bag in the car – just in case."

She stood. "Let me grab a couple backpacks. We can make piles and then put them right in the backpacks."

When Riley finished emptying the box, he had three piles. Each pile contained mylar blankets, wool socks, two Lifestraws, a cheap plastic poncho, a pocket knife, a bic lighter, a wind-up radio, a small roll of paracord, duct tape, and a compass.

"It doesn't look like much when you lay it all out like that," Allison said. "I guess I wasn't as ready as I thought."

"You were obviously readier than most people." Riley started stuffing items in each backpack.

The basement door opened at the top of the stairs. Two pairs of feet hurried down the steps. Jaden and Beth reached the bottom on the stairs.

"Allison," Jaden said. "Mary wants to know if you have any card tables down here or if we should carry the food to the bunkhouse to eat."

"There are a couple card tables and chairs right over there." Allison pointed to the far wall. "Riley and I will bring them up. I think we need a break from this."

She looked at Riley. "I've got some medicine to make tomorrow, but if you're free the next day, I'd love some more help here."

Riley shook his head. "I'm leaving with Will tomorrow. We might be gone for one day or three. Won't know until we are heading home. But, if the work is still here when I get back, I'd be happy to help."

Allison

Bowls of food lined the counter in the kitchen. Allison wiped the folding tables. Jaden followed with silverware and festive napkins. The plates sat piled near the food.

"Let's get the little ones fed first," Mary called. Mothers led the youngest children to the counter and helped with adding food to the plates. Older children followed. They giggled as they took turns.

"Gotta love a good smorgasbord," Riley leaned over and whispered in Allison's ear.

She grinned.

He let her go in front of him at the end of the line and then followed her to the only remaining empty seats. Several pair of eyes watched curiously.

He thought about reaching out and touching her, just to give those enquiring minds something to think about, but held back. This was something that he would do for Will.

He turned his head to look around the room. Where was Will?

The back door opened. Megan stepped inside. She slid off her jacket and hung it on the hook by the back door. When she turned back to the room, her eyes landed on Riley and a flush crept onto her cheeks. She looked at the floor before straightening her back and walking to the counter where she filled a plate.

She carried it across the room and sat on the sofa, balancing the plate on her knees.

"Where's Will?" Riley called across the room.

She became busy moving food around her plate. "I don't know." She shrugged, but didn't raise her face. "Jensen came and picked up that Peters guy an hour and a half ago." She turned to Allison. "Jensen said to tell you that he'd be out tomorrow to go over the gas rationing rules. And, if things go well, in about a week, we should also have a couple grocery deliveries and there will be rationing books for those as well."

The room fell silent before everyone began talking at once. "Finally!" Mary crossed her hands over her breasts. "Thank you, God! They are starting to pull us out of the stone age!"

"Yeah, if Phillips doesn't block deliveries and come after the rest of us," Rolly muttered.

The room got silent as people resumed eating.

Riley turned back to Megan. "What was Will doing

after that Peters guy left?"

Her fork clattered to the floor. She picked it up.

"What's your problem?" she snapped.

Riley cringed. "I'm sorry. I'll finish my food here and fix him a plate."

"Good idea." She bent over her plate, letting her straight hair provide a curtain in front of her face.

"Leave your plate here," Allison said when he'd eaten his last bite and leaned back in his chair. "Go fix Will a plate and take it to him."

"Thanks." He pushed back his chair and went to the counter where he piled a plate with ham, green beans and mashed potatoes.

Will was bent over the table. He stared at a map of Illinois. He smiled when he looked up and saw the plate that Riley carried. "Thanks, man."

"What are we looking at?" Riley asked.

"The route to Springfield. Looks like it will be Highway 26 as far as Peoria and then I-74 for a few miles before we pick up I-155. From what Jensen said, the FEMA office is south of Lincoln. Peters told me that Phillips's men don't venture any further north than a little town of Williamsville except for the spies Phillips stations out there."

He pointed at a mark on the map. "Here is Williamsville. Peters said that the best way in would be on the east side." He pointed to a mark in the middle of Springfield. "Here is the governor's mansion. That's where he said Phillips is staying. And here," he said pointing to another mark. "This is the capitol building. A lot of the women and children are kept there. He thinks they are in the basement. His wife isn't there. She's over here."

He drug his finger toward the bottom of the map. "It used to be a Catholic high school. The women are walked across the street to the church every morning to work and then walked back every evening where they are locked in until morning."

"How do you plan on getting close to Phillips?" Riley snagged a slice of ham from the plate and took a bite.

"I have no doubt he will welcome me with open arms. The death of his brother was hard on him. I was the only one who was willing to go the distance with him. And I did go the distance." He reached across and picked up a slice of ham.

"No cheese?"

"I didn't see any."

"Damn, I wish Mary would make some more."

"I think Mary is busy with other things. I heard her telling Jaden that when they get the root cellar built, she'll be making more cheese."

"Yum." He folded the slice of ham in half and shoved the whole chunk into his mouth. With bulging cheeks, he mumbled a sentence.

"What?" Riley said. "I didn't quite get that."

Will chewed a bit more and then swallowed. "I said that it's a good thing this isn't chicken. You're probably tired of chicken." He grinned showing ham stuck in his teeth.

Riley rolled his eyes. "You just have to push it, don't you?"

Will shrugged. "I just like the look on your face when you've had enough. You get this little wrinkle across the bridge of your nose and then your cheek starts twitching." He chuckled.

"Whatever," Riley said as he grabbed another slice of ham and bit off a chunk. "Were you going to share that you did the nasty with Megan?"

Will stopped chewing and looked Riley in the eyes. "Don't go there," he said.

"Go where? Nothing is off limits to you, but I'm not allowed to talk about certain things? That's not fair."

"It might not be fair, but we aren't going there with Megan. Leave her out of the fun and games."

Riley gazed at Will. "You're serious about her, aren't you?"

"I am."

"For how long?"

"A while."

"I just spent several days and nights in close quarters with you guys. I never noticed a thing."

"We were on a mission."

"Huh! Just when you think you know someone so well, they gotta blind side you. Well, congratulations on finding love during the apocalypse. I hope everything works out for you guys."

"Thanks." Will reached out and clamped his hand on Riley's shoulder. "And I apologize for going overboard on the chicken jokes earlier. I think I just wanted to wind you up in front of Megan."

"Yeah, well you did."

"I know. I'm sorry."

Riley smiled. "Let's get this trip planned. What time are we leaving?"

"It'll be late afternoon. Jensen is going to deliver the truck out here. Unless we run into problems, we should reach Springfield around 9pm."

"Traveling after dark? Are you comfortable with that?"

"We'll have FEMA escorts for most of the way. They say that the roads are pretty safe – and even if they aren't, we are used to this. It's what we thrive on. Right?"

"Right." Riley grabbed the last slice of ham and shoved it in his mouth.

"Hey!" Will stared at the plate. "I thought you brought that plate for me!"

"I saved you the mashed potatoes and veggies, didn't I?" Riley licked his fingers.

"Thanks." Will shook his head before picking up the plate. Holding it in his left hand, he twirled the green beans into the mashed potatoes and took a bite.

The door slammed open. Ten-year-old Erin Grant

held it wide so Jaden could step in with a box of clean laundry. Erin's brother Cody followed carrying another box. Sasha Wolff also carried a load.

Behind them, laughing and talking, the remainder of the children entered. They were followed by their mothers, who upon seeing Riley and Will bent over the map, shushed the children.

"Come on guys," Lisa Grant called. "Let's go on back to the corner and play a game of 'Win, Lose, or Draw.' Then it'll be time to get ready for bed."

"We're done here." Will folded the map before scooping the last of the mashed potatoes and green beans into his mouth.

"Come on," he said motioning to Riley. "I want to get this plate back to Allison."

Will

The morning sun filtered through the new leaves bursting from buds. A slight breeze sent shadows dancing across the yard.

Riley and Will sat at the picnic table next to the barn. Riley used a whetstone, running the edge of his knife smoothly along the stone.

Will's bag lay open in front of him. He pulled each item out and sorted them into two piles.

"What are you doing?" Megan slid onto the bench next to him.

"Sorting my stuff. When I go in, I have to look like I've been rode hard and put up wet. And I can't keep stuff like this." He held up his tactical communication headset. "No one traveling by themselves would have a reason to carry this. That would be something that would make Phillips wonder who had the other set."

"Does Phillips know that you were law enforcement?"

Will nodded. "Yes, he knows. As soon as I got the job, he started asking me if I wanted him to pull some strings and get me promoted."

"Well." She picked up the headset and turned it over in her hand. "What if you had two sets in your bag? If he checks your bag and asks, you can just tell him that you kept them in case you ever had a need to use them. Then, Riley can keep track of you while you are separated."

Riley felt a smile form on his lips. He looked up at Will and grinned. "Nothing like having someone with brains handy."

Will put his arm around Megan's shoulder and pulled her close before planting a kiss on the top of her head. "Great idea! Thanks!" he said.

Megan blushed. The smile that crossed her face was full of pride. She glanced at Riley who gave her the thumbs up.

"Want to do me a favor?" Will asked her.

"Happy to," she replied.

"When the girls did laundry last night, they washed all my clothes too. I can have one pair of clean clothes, but I can't show up all spiffy with all clean clothes. Could you take these two pair of jeans and these shirts and drag them around the arena? I need them to look like I've been living out of my bag.

"Okay, but that seems a little extreme. Are you sure you can't just tell him that you found a house with an old fashioned wringer washer?"

Riley snorted.

"That's another great idea, but I think I'd rather not give him too many things to question."

"Yeah, you're right. Give me the clothes. I'll dirty them up for you."

When she was gone, Riley looked up from the knife he was sharpening. "How did you convince her to stay behind?" he asked.

Will shrugged. "I didn't have to convince her. We talked yesterday afternoon and I explained how hard missions like this could be and that it would be much easier for me if I went in knowing that you had my back and I didn't have to worry about her. And, if she were here with Allison, it would ease my mind about leaving Allison and the group alone."

"I'm glad you guys found each other."

"Me too," Will replied. "I've been impressed with her determination from the day she announced she was going to join the security team. She worked hard to get on the team and she never disappointed me."

"Oh, I agree. She has spunk. You guys will do just

fine." He set down the whetstone. "Hand me that gun cleaning kit."

By the time Megan returned, the bag had been repacked and was sitting on the table between the men. Will rolled the clothes up and shoved them into the side of the bag.

"Can I get you guys some coffee?" she asked.

Riley stood. "I'll get the coffee. You sit down."

"Thanks," she smiled, settling in close to Will.

Jensen showed up with the truck a few minutes after noon. Lunch had been served. Riley, Will and Megan had opted to eat at the outdoor picnic table and discuss the trip.

Jensen exited the truck and strolled to the table. "I'll need a lift back to town. I have to talk to Allison before I leave, but come on over and let me show you what we have."

The truck was a 1978 Ford Supercab. With two-tone paint – dark brown on top and light brown on the bottom. The topper was painted dark brown to match the truck. Window tint had been applied to the topper windows making seeing inside the bed of the truck almost impossible. Jensen opened the tailgate of the truck.

The Yamaha enduro bike in the back had new tires.

"Two-stroke," Riley said kneeling inside the bed of the truck. "Do you have to use premix?"

"It's got an autolube system so you can fill up with gas anywhere. No worry about premixing. The speedometer and tachometer have been stripped. It's a 250. Ground clearance is not quite ten inches." He looked up at Will. "Do you have any dirt bike experience?"

"Yeah, I've done my share of trail riding. It's been a couple years, but if I need to go off roading, I'll be fine."

"Good to hear. The guys built that box along the passenger side. It holds four five-gallon gas cans. You probably won't need them, but I don't want you stranded anywhere."

He scratched his head. "All right, when I sent my guys down to Lincoln yesterday, they had strict orders not to tell anyone what they were scouting for. In case Phillips has spies inside FEMA, I don't want him finding out that someone is coming for him. They stopped in Peoria and told the Commander that Phillips is planning an attack on Monday. The Commander was aware of Phillips's raiders. He'd heard that Phillips had something big planned, but didn't know what it was."

He closed the tailgate of the truck. "When my guys got to the Lincoln office, they told them the same story. The guys in Lincoln knew a little more than the guys in Peoria. They had heard that Phillips was planning an attack but they didn't know where or when. They've actually been planning a raid. My guys asked them to hold off until they'd talked to you. They also asked for a safe house to use tonight and tomorrow. Here's the address." He handed them a piece of paper with an address and a crude map.

"It's south of Lincoln, just outside Phillips's perimeter. You will stay there tonight. The Commander and two of his men will meet you there at five tomorrow morning."

He turned toward the bunkhouse. "I need to go over the ration books with Allison and the adults. I also have some information from Springfield that I'd like to share."

Allison

The children were gathered at the back of the common room, studying. Lisa Grant was at the whiteboard writing multiplication problems on the board. Jaden and Paul sat with the younger kids, helping them when they had questions. Bella sat next to Jaden.

Will found Allison and Mary in the store room going through a box of vegetable seeds.

"Hey," he said. "Jensen is here. He's got some things he wants to talk about."

Allison frowned. "I'll see if Jaden and Paul will take the kids to the arena for some kickball or something. Mary, would you go to the house and see if there are any adults there that want to hear what Mr. Jensen has to say?"

Allison set the water pot on the stove and brought down containers of herbs. She brought cups and honey to the tables. The water had just come to a boil when the door opened and Mary entered with the men who had been in the house resting from security duty.

Allison pointed to each herb container. "Choose

whichever you want. We have plenty of honey. Take as much as you want."

Jensen stood at the front of the room. "First I want to go over the gas rationing. In a couple weeks, we'll have deliveries of sugar and salt and other commodities," he said.

He took a drink of his tea before continuing. "These gas stamps are for five gallons at a time. You may use up to four stamps per visit. There is only one station in town selling gas. That's John's on Elm Street. When you go in to get gas, you will sign and then hand over the stamps that you are using. The employee who pumps your gas is also required to sign the stamp before he pumps your gas. The price of gas today is $4.00 a gallon. That might fluctuate a little each day, but should not fluctuate much."

He looked around the room. "If you do not have cash to pay for gas, you can stop at the FEMA office and barter. We are always happy to trade for food or ammo or just about anything." He laughed. "Day before yesterday I bought a bottle of Vodka from a guy in town so he could buy his gas."

"I've given all the books to Allison this time. You will have to decide amongst yourselves if that is how you want to handle things. The alternative would be for each family to come into the office and register as an individual family. You would then be given your rationing books in your name.

"At the beginning of next month, I will have new books for you. Any stamps you have not used in this month's books must be turned in when you are issued the next book.

"We should also have commodities. I can't tell you what they will be, but there will be at least sugar and flour. There will likely be cooking oil. The stamps for those will work similar to the gas stamps. When you use them, you will need to sign the stamp you are using and watch the grocer sign as well. You might find that the prices for food might be a little cheaper than you have paid in the past."

Greta Burke raised her hand. "So with the gas and the food, we need stamps plus money to buy?"

"That's right," Jensen said. "The way it was explained to me was that it will work very similar to rationing during World War II. Each person can buy a set amount – but you do have to pay for it. This isn't a freebie program. You are issued stamps so that everyone has a fair amount. People with money can't hoard food and create a shortage. And, if you don't have money, remember that you can come by my office. We will barter with you. Or, to put it in plain English, we will buy whatever you need to sell to come up with the money to buy food.

"The ration stamps will be issued once a month but they are for specific weeks. Each stamp in the book will have a set of dates that the stamp will be good for. The weeks will run from Saturday midnight to the following Saturday midnight.

"Any more questions?" He looked around the room.

"What if we don't need the commodities?" Allison asked. "I know that there are a few things that we most definitely would love to have, but for the most part, we've done very well with making our own stuff. Can we donate our stamps to another family?"

Jensen shook his head. "No, what you don't use can't be given away or sold. I would encourage you to purchase what has been allocated to you."

He looked around the room again. "Any more questions?"

When no one stepped forward, he continued. "The last thing I need to address with you before I have Will and Shane take me back to the office and start their journey is this: the government is looking for local farmers to grow large quantities of specific food. They would like to form a partnership with the farmers in which the government will supply the seeds and allocate extra gasoline. In return, the government will collect the food at harvest and redistribute it where needed."

Allison frowned. "You mean they want farmers to do all the labor and then they just swoop in and pick up the food?"

"Well, they would be supplying the seeds and the gasoline for your equipment. And, they will let you keep enough for personal use, of course."

"No deal," said Allison. "We will plant our own seeds and we will plant enough to help supply the town, but with all due respect, we don't want to partner with the government. Will that be a problem?"

"Not at all. In fact," he said with a grin. "I agree with you. I had to ask. It's my job. If you have the seeds and the labor, I'd much prefer to buy my local produce from you. We'll find a way to buy or barter. Can we plan on getting together someday soon to discuss what we can realistically expect from you?"

"Of course." Allison nodded. "I'll get with Mary and we will have something for you in a week or two."

He nodded, then picked up his cup and drained the last of his tea. He turned to Will. "Are you guys ready?"

Will stood, walked over to Megan and wrapped her

in his arms. The common room erupted in cheers.

"It's about time," Rolly shouted.

"Wondered when you two would smarten up." Sam Smith chortled.

Lisa Grant and Karen Funderburg clapped and said, "Awww."

Will planted a kiss on the top of Megan's head, then pulled back and gazed into her eyes. "Be safe," he said.

"You too," she replied. She looked around the room and grinned.

"Come on," Riley said. "Let's do this."

At the FEMA office, Jensen took them to his office where he lifted a folder from his desk. "Here are the transcripts of our interviews with Matthews and his men. We made a point to interview only the top three guys. But," he grinned. "they think Peters is dead. I've got him in the city jail and he has given us a lot of things he didn't even realize he knew. I just needed someone who was skilled at asking questions. The transcripts of his interviews are in there too."

"Do you guys need anything?"

"Don't think so."

"Okay then. When you get to Lincoln, you'll have to fill Commander Jacobs in. We didn't tell them anything other than Phillips was getting ready for an attack on FEMA offices and on Illinois borders. If Phillips has any men inside FEMA, we didn't want it leaked."

"Thanks, man. Let's hope I get in and out fast. I've promised Allison that I'd help with building the root cellar. I'd much rather be doing that than this."

Riley

The map led Riley and Will to an exit at Elkhart, then several miles on county roads to a homestead surrounded by trees. The closest neighbor appeared to be about a mile away.

"Let me out here," Will said. "Go down the road to give me time to scope this."

Ten minutes later, Riley pulled off the county road into the driveway. The house, a white two story with green shutters, sat about a hundred feet off the road. Will stood on the front porch. He motioned for Riley to park in the garage and moved to lift the overhead door.

"Key was right where the note said it would be," Will told Riley after he had backed the truck into the garage and shut off the engine. "Kitchen and living room have black paper on the windows and flashlights were on the kitchen counter. Looks like we are set."

Riley opened the tailgate and leaned in to pull out the box of food. Will waited until he'd stepped away to pull out the two extra backpacks. He closed the tailgate and followed Riley into the kitchen.

"It'll be dark in a few hours. I'm going to go out

and nose around the property. Can you keep an eye on the road and driveway?"

"Sure. Where are the comms?"

"Got them here." He slid the earbud into his ear and laid Riley's on the counter. "Gonna start supper while I'm out?"

"I think it's your turn to cook."

Will gazed at him for a moment before saying, "I could agree with you, but then we'd both be wrong."

Riley laughed. "Did you pack anything good?"

"Of course. There's a can of tuna and some mac and cheese. Mix 'em together and I'll be a happy man."

"Boy, Megan's got an easy life in front of her."

Will winked and pointed a finger at Riley and opened the back door. "Catch you later, Alligator."

Riley shook his head. "What is wrong with you?"

"Lots of things," Will replied. "Want a list?" He closed the door before Riley could comment.

Between watching the road for traffic and setting up the propane burner, Riley had macaroni and cheese with tuna ready in less than an hour. For good measure he added a small can of peas he found in the food box.

"Smells good," Will said, slamming the back door behind him. "Let's eat and then go over the things that Peters shared with us."

The map of Springfield showed the governor's mansion which was where Peters claimed Phillips was living. Several blocks away, the Capitol Building was where Peters claimed many of the women and children were being held.

Will slid his index finger lower on the map. "Down here is where Peters said they are holding his wife. They sleep in the old school and walk them across the street to the church every morning to work. Peters said that there are at least three or four more setups like this but he wasn't sure exactly how many or where they are located."

Riley scratched his head. "So how do you plan to sneak in, kill Phillips, and rescue Peters's wife when you don't even know where all the women and children are being held?"

"First, I'm not going to sneak in. I'm riding in on that bike in the garage. When I get stopped, I'm going to tell them that I'm there to see Phillips and if it takes some convincing, so be it. Once I get to Phillips, I kill him and then head south to the school. Those people in the capitol building are going to have to wait."

"Are you planning on asking the local FEMA for help when they show up in the morning? What was the name of the guy that's coming?"

Will frowned. "I can't remember the guy's name, but yeah, I'm open to any suggestions they have. We'll find out in the morning if they have any intel to share. My plan is to leave immediately after talking to them, just in case Phillips has someone on the inside of FEMA who might get word to him"

"Have you picked the route you're going to take into town?"

"I have. I'll leave here and hit this county road. That will turn into State Road 124. I'll either go through or around the golf course depending on what I find. Then, North Peoria Road will lead me to within a few blocks of the mansion. I'm going to ride right up to the gates. I'm sure they will have guards. I'll play that by ear."

"They'll take your guns."

"They can have my guns."

"And you plan on getting in and out as fast as possible."

"Well, I don't plan on having a beer with him."

"Five in the morning will be here before we know it. Who is taking first watch?"

"I will." Will left the map on the table and moved to the front of the house.

Jaden Makes Mayonnaise

Allison stood at the counter in front of the window. She reached up and lifted the parsley off the shelf and set it on the counter. She carefully snipped the outer portions of the plant before setting the pot back on the sill.

"Can I help?" Jaden called from the back of the room.

Allison turned and smiled. "Are there kids that need your help back there?"

Allison heard a snort. "No. She's a slave driver. Please put her to work," eight-year-old Cody Grant muttered. The group of children doing schoolwork giggled.

"Come on," Allison said. "I'm going to dry this parsley and store it for later."

"We haven't seen any seeds from the parsley. Doesn't it have seeds?"

"It does, honey. But I just planted this eight months ago. Parsley doesn't go to seed until the second year. That's something that we'll be doing next year."

"Oh. How do you remember all this stuff?

Everything is different and you use them for different things but you always know what to do with each thing and what it helps with. How can you remember all that? I can't."

"You remember a lot, sweetheart. Remember, I've been doing this for many, many years. The first couple of years I couldn't do it without looking in my notes. And, even now, I have to look at my notes quite often. If it's not something that I do on a regular basis, I need to look it up. That's why we always keep good notes. Notes help you remember things you don't do often and notes also help when another person has to do a job that you've always done."

"Yeah. Maybe someday I'll remember more than I do now."

Allison pointed to a cutting board. "Can you hand me that board?"

She laid the parsley out and expertly chopped it into small bits.

"I need you to teach me how to do that too."

"The trick here," said Allison, "is curling the fingers to keep your fingertips away from the knife. Use your knuckles as a guide for the knife. Here." She handed the knife to Jaden and moved out of the way. "You do it. Take slow, even strokes using your knuckles as a guide."

Jaden followed the instructions. When she sped up, Allison stopped her. "Now is not the time for speed. Now is the time to learn skill. Speed will come later."

"Sorry," said Jaden.

"No need to be sorry. We just want you to be safe. Speed will come. Trust me."

They were laying the bits out on the fine screen when the back door opened and Mary stepped in.

"It feels like rain out there." She removed her jacket and set a basket of eggs on the counter. "Jaden, you want to help me make mayonnaise?"

"Sure, but I've watched you make mayonnaise lots of times. I think I know how."

Mary smiled. "What are our ingredients?"

Jaden scrunched her nose. "I think 2 eggs, a little bit of lemon juice, a dash of salt and some olive oil. I think you use powdered mustard sometimes too."

"Okay. Do you want to try it on your own, or do you want me to walk you through it and explain what we are doing?"

"Can you tell me what to do and let me do it?" Jaden jumped up and down making her hair bounce around her face.

"I can. And I will try to teach you the science of making it. It's so simple to make if you understand the process. Can you go get the pie pan?"

Jaden ran to the cupboard and brought back an aluminum pie tin.

"No, honey. We don't want to use aluminum or copper because they will make the mayonnaise off color. Let's use that glass pie pan I always use. I like to use it for two reasons. The first is that my mayonnaise won't be off color. And the second reason is, I like the weight of the glass pan. It helps me control it a little better."

When Jaden returned with the glass pan, Mary pointed to the tall stool next to the counter. "We're going to put a dish towel down under the pie pan to help hold it in place. Then we want to get those two eggs you said we needed and we are just going to use the yolks. Can you separate them?"

Jaden did as she was told. "I would have made it wrong because I forgot that you separated the eggs."

"Actually," Mary said. "you can use whole eggs if

you want. You just have to double all the other ingredients."

"Another thing," Mary said as she picked up the egg shells and put them in the compost bucket. "Use the freshest eggs you can get. The fresher the egg, the better the mayo. Fresh egg yolks seem to blend with the oil better than older eggs. I also like to use room temperature eggs and oil.

"Okay, you have your egg yolks. I'm going to let you decide where you are more comfortable. I like to put the pan on my lap because once you start whisking, you have to keep going for a while and my arm gets sore if I'm reaching over the counter. You decide where you want to do it."

Jaden looked at the pie pan on the counter. "Maybe I'll leave it there. I'm afraid I'll drop it if I hold it."

"I just set the pan on my lap and hold it with my free hand, and then stir the mayonnaise with my other hand. You just get comfy wherever you want. And, when you are ready, start stirring the lemon juice into it. If you don't have lemon juice, you can use vinegar. And let's put our salt in as well."

Jaden used a fork to stir the egg and lemon juice.

"What is happening in this step is you are using the egg you to act as an emulsifier. An emulsifier is something that helps one liquid blend with another."

Mary looked up. Allison was leaning over the counter watching.

"Keep going," Allison said. "I've never heard that before."

Mary smiled. "Okay. Think about vinegar and oil. You've made simple salad dressings before. It's basically vinegar and oil. You shake it up to mix it. But after it sits for a few minutes, it starts to separate."

Allison nodded.

"Our egg is our emulsifier. It helps bind the vinegar or lemon juice and the oil. So what Jaden is doing in this step is blending the lemon juice and egg yolk."

"How long do I have to stir this?" Jaden asked.

Mary looked down at the egg mixture. "You've got it blended really nice. Now it's time to start adding the oil. We will use about a cup and a half of olive oil. Any oil will work. Some people don't like olive oil because they think its too strong of a flavor, but I use olive oil."

She brought the oil closer to Jaden. "This is critical. It will make or break your mayonnaise. I start with just one or two little drops of oil and whisk it in.

Then a few more drops. Whisk that in. If you do
this slowly, you will get a thick, rich mayonnaise.
Add the oil too fast and you will get greasy egg
yolk."

She watched as Jaden added more oil and stirred.
"Each time you add oil and blend, it should get a
little thicker."

She leaned over to get a closer look. "That is
beautiful, Jaden. You can start adding just a little
more oil at a time now, but not too much. Keep
whisking. See how it's starting to feel like instant
pudding? It's starting to get thicker. If we were
going to add mustard or anything else, this is when I
would add it."

When all the oil had been added, Jaden said, "My
arm is killing me. Can I stop now?"

"Yes, dear. You've just made a perfect mayonnaise.
Most people don't get it perfect their first try. You
did! You should be proud."

Jaden grinned. "Thank you," she said.

Mary took the mayonnaise, dipped her finger into it
and tasted it. "Yum! That is perfect!"

She set the pan on the counter. "So you've made
mayonnaise. Now, if you wanted, you could add
some of that parsley you were chopping, or any

other herb. You could make egg salad or potato salad. I sometimes add just a little horseradish. We can even make ranch dressing. But, for now, we have mayonnaise that you made all by yourself."

Jaden stood and shook her arm. "Boy, my arm is so tired!"

"If you did this every day, your arm wouldn't be tired at all. Remember when we made butter the first time and you had to shake the jar for such a long time?"

"Yeah. After the first couple of times making butter, I wasn't so tired."

"That's the way everything in life is. It might be hard at first, but once you get used to it, it's not hard anymore."

Will

The aroma of fresh coffee filled the kitchen of the farmhouse north of Springfield.

Will stepped out of the bedroom. He shrugged on the shirt Megan had dirtied up for him.

"Damn! She was serious getting these clothes dirty. They are nasty!" He buttoned the flannel shirt.

Riley threw back his head and laughed. "I think she dragged it through horse shit."

Will's mouth opened. He looked down at his pants. "Where?"

"There, just under your knees." Riley pointed.

"Aww, man! I can smell it."

"Well, you did tell her you wanted to look like you'd been sleeping in a barn."

"Yea, but I'd rather not smell like it too."

"It seals your cover story. You don't smell too bad. Have some coffee." He poured the dark coffee into a metal cup.

They were just finishing their oatmeal when a gray Ford Explorer turned off the road and stopped at the end of the driveway.

"Stay inside," Will said over his shoulder. He stepped onto the porch and waited.

The Explorer moved toward the house, coming to a stop near the front porch.

A tall man with graying hair stepped out of the passenger side. "My name is Commander James Ulcher with Federal Emergency Management Agency. I am looking for a man named Riley."

"He's inside," Will replied. "Come on in."

Ulcher leaned into the vehicle and said something. The back door opened and a younger man with close cropped hair stepped out. Together they approached the house and climbed the steps.

Riley waited in the kitchen. He poured two more cups of coffee and slid them across the counter before looking at Ulcher.

"Shane Riley," he said.

Ulcher gazed across the counter. "Commander Jensen is a good man. I served with him. I trust his judgement, but I have no idea why I am here."

He picked up his coffee and took a sip. "Yesterday he sends three guys down. They tell me that Phillips is planning a big event but they refuse to tell me what it is. They say that Shane Riley will be down today to fill me in."

"And, here I am." Riley reached his hand across the counter. Ulcher hesitated before committing to the handshake.

"Okay." Ulcher sighed. "Tell me what's so secret that I couldn't have been told yesterday morning."

Riley looked at Will. "Will can fill you in," he told Ulcher.

Will offered his hand, which Ulcher shook. "William Mead, Winnebago County SWAT team leader – well at least I was before the shit hit the fan."

Will turned to the younger man who had followed Ulcher in. "And you are?" he asked.

The man stepped forward and offered his hand. "Jim Reynolds. Public Information Officer."

Will set his coffee cup on the counter and opened the map. "Two days ago," he said, "we foiled an attempt to raid our community. The perpetrators planned on kidnapping everyone and hauling them here, to Springfield. The women and children would be separated from the adult men and forced to work in various positions. The men would be used as soldiers. Phillips keeps them in line by threatening to kill their families if they don't do what he wants."

Ulcher nodded. "We knew this. We have identified nine buildings the women and children are being kept in. We are ready to move in and free them. Once they are free, the men should be able to escape."

Will said, "This was supposed to be their last trip for rounding up citizens. On Monday, they are planning the next phase."

"Which is?"

"Blowing up the Illinois FEMA offices and camps. Then blowing all bridges across the Mississippi River to isolate the state. On the east border of the state, they planned patrols."

Ulcher nodded. "We had heard of the blowing bridges. Had not heard of the FEMA attacks. They won't get into ours. We're ready for any attack."

"Are you ready for a dirty bomb?"

"Why the hell would they set off a dirty bomb? They don't do any immediate damage other than the explosion. The dirty part of it takes a while to kill.

That just doesn't make sense."

"Nothing Phillips is doing make a lot of sense. And I'd like to know how he got so many followers that he was able to pull this off."

"Well, Logan Correctional was right down the road. It was an all-female facility. There were 1,500 prisoners there. Jacksonville and Taylorville aren't too far away. They were minimum security centers so I'd say that most of the inmates weren't too hardened. But I'd say most of his followers were broken out of Menard Maximum Security Correctional Center. It held almost 3,000 inmates. Once he broke them out, they were his. From what I've heard, if they weren't with him, he killed them."

He lifted his cup and drained the last of it. "I didn't get assigned here until two months after the flare. Phillips was already hunkered in. His men had run off or killed any decent civilians and hauled out the dead. Springfield actually is operating as a normal town – if a crazed dictator could be called normal."

"Do you realize that they have an observation post on a hill above your headquarters?" Will asked.

"Yeah, we know. That's why we normally have a couple decoys. When we left this morning, two trucks with FEMA decals had left shortly before us.

They each went a different way when they got out to the highway. By the time I left, their spies were busy keeping track of where the trucks went."

He held his cup out. "Got any more?"

Riley lifted the pot and filled the cup.

"Thanks." He turned back to Will. "So why are you guys here? What's the big secret?"

"I'm here to take Phillips out."

"Ain't going to happen." Ulcher shook his head. "He's holed up in the mansion and he's got ten or fifteen men protecting him. You won't even get close."

"Ah." Will held up his finger. "I've got a way in."

"What's that?"

"Phillips and I are buddies."

"What?"

"Phillips's younger brother and I were best friends. We hung around with Phillips when we were kids. He was a whack job back then too, but he was like family. When we went off to college, his brother and I were roommates. We still hung out with Phillips a lot. One night we were out partying and there was a shooting. Phillips's brother was killed. I think that's when Phillips stepped off the deep end. I stayed by his side and helped him track down the gangbanger who killed his brother. He will welcome me. I can get to him."

"So, what's your plan?"

"I'm just going to ride up to the mansion and knock on the gate."

"That won't work." Ulcher shook his head. "The men at the gates won't let you get close. They don't know you and they aren't going to let a stranger close to their meal ticket."

"I can be very persuasive," Will said. "I've got to try. If I don't, things won't get better. They'll get a lot worse."

Ulcher sighed. "I just don't want to see another good man lost to that dictator. When do you plan on going in? I can move some of my troops into position to help."

"I'm leaving just as soon as we finish talking."

"No!" Ulcher insisted. "I need time to get my troops in position."

"If I give you time to do that, any of his spies would have time to get word to him that someone was going to try to get to him. Once I take care of him, his men will be running in circles, that would be a good time for you to move in."

"What are your plans for getting out alive?"

"I made a promise to a man. The man's wife is in a school south and west of the mansion. After I get away from the mansion, I'm heading straight to that school and rescuing his wife. Then I'll get her out of the city."

"That guy a friend of yours?"

"No, but he's the one who gave me all the intel I needed to do what I have to do. I made a promise and I keep my promises."

"Do you realize that there are at least eight more building with hostages? You could be condemning those hostages."

"If there is more I can do, I will. But I start with what needs to be done and a promise I made."

"I can help." Ulcher leaned over the map and pointed to a road near the top. "Here is where we are right now."

He drug his finger to an intersecting road. "This would be your best way to the mansion. Phillips hasn't put much along here. This road skirts the golf course and there is nothing worth his time along there until you get closer to the capitol. It would take you about twenty minutes from here."

He moved his finger to a point east of their current location. "This is my office. It would take me about fifteen minutes to get back there from here. Another half hour to round up my troops. And then another half hour or so to get them in place."

He looked up at Will to see if he was getting through before continuing. "I understand your hesitation to give someone a chance to warn Phillips. But I want to help you. And, I'd like to take this opportunity to take out as many of Phillips's men as possible. What I'd like to do is let you do what you want to do. But, as soon as you've gotten inside, I'd like to attack the perimeter. It would draw his men away while you headed to the school."

Will stared at the map, and scratched the stubble on his chin.

"Where would you attack from?"

Ulcher pointed at two spots on the map. "Since we are limited in setup time, these two spots are the easiest to approach and get into position. We can be in position before Phillips's men can assemble. Then we work our way in street by street. We've done drills and we can do this."

He stared at the map. "The scenarios that we've drilled for have been to take the town street by street, working our way toward the mansion. We can deviate from our plans just a little and target three of the buildings that hostages are in. The rest will have to be taken after we've put down Phillips's men."

He raised his eyes. "How confident are you that you will be able to take him out?"

"I can take him out."

"They'll take your guns before you go inside – if they let you inside."

"I don't need my guns."

Ulcher stared at the map before raising his head. "All right," he sighed. "I need an hour and a half."

"Can't do it. I need to get inside before any potential spies can warn him. Once I get inside, I can take my time." He leaned against the counter. "How sure are you on your timeline? Can you get your men in place in an hour and a half?"

"Most definitely."

"Then how about we try this." He leaned forward. "It'll take me twenty minutes to get there. It might take five minutes to get inside. It might take forty-five minutes. But if I can get in there and assume that you'll be in place when you say you will be, I can use your movement to create confusion. It will make it easier for me to escape if they are going nuts. But, no matter what, if you haven't attacked in an hour and a half, I'm going ahead with my plan."

"Understood." He turned to the younger man who had followed him in. "Jim, how many men do we have in the barracks right now that I can activate in just a few minutes?"

"Eighty-five," Jim replied. "And twelve more that will be coming off security detail in about ten minutes."

Ulcher leaned over the map again. "I'm going to send four teams of ten in to each of these hostage buildings." He pointed to four spots on the map. "We will be getting in before they move the women and children to the work areas so hopefully they will be safe while we take over. The remaining fifty-seven men will come with me."

He looked up at Will. "I will only tell my men that we are moving on our plans that we've been drilling for. Only after the fighting starts will I give my men a heads up that there is a good guy in the mansion. Our mission is to take no prisoners. We will be taking out as many of Phillips's men as we can."

Will nodded. "That's the only way to do it. We can't let them run so they can set up somewhere else and do the same thing."

Riley

"What about him?" Ulcher nodded his head toward Riley.

"The plan was to leave him here. I can't take him to meet Phillips and once hell breaks loose, I need to head straight down to rescue that woman."

Riley stepped to the counter. "Commander Ulcher, you should have answers to a couple questions I have." He pointed at a road that circled around the west side of town. "This Highway 4. How well patrolled is that?"

Ulcher shook his head. "They don't usually wander west of that highway. But that's the border to the town and they do keep it clear. Depending on their mood for the day, we've seen them let vehicles through and we've seen them take out vehicles. So, if that's a route that you are thinking about taking, I'd reconsider."

He pointed at a road five miles east of the highway. "Now, this road would be a better bet. Follow it down almost to Interstate 72. About a quarter mile north of that interstate, Bunker Hill Road will take you to Wabash Avenue. The problem is, you are visible from their checkpoints on the Interstate all the way in to town. If you could get that far, MacArthur Boulevard will take you a couple of blocks from the hostages you friend is trying to rescue."

"What are you thinking?" Will had moved in to follow Ulcher's directions.

Riley looked up. "I'm thinking that when you leave, I can work my way around the city and come in from the southwest corner. Once you take out Phillips and get to the hostages, I can meet you there with the truck."

"What if you get stopped?"

"Then I'll tell them that I've got a warning for Phillips. Uhm. I'll tell them that soldiers are moving in from the west." Riley rubbed the back of his head. "I'll think of something…"

"Actually, I think that's a good idea." Ulcher leaned across the map. "If they think there are soldiers coming in from the west, we'll easily flank them from the east. The biggest danger is going to be getting you from the mansion to the hostages without getting killed in the crossfire."

"Don't worry about me." Will stared at the map. "You know," he said, "I've always believed in the rule that the best plan is the simplest plan. But this has some merits. Considering that once you guys move in, I won't know the good guys from the bad guys and I still have to make it about a mile to the hostage building, it might be a good thing to have you coming up from the southwest in the truck." He scratched his nose and looked at Riley. "Is there anything you need from me?"

Riley shook his head. "Nope. I'll try to be near the hostage building in about an hour and a half. I should be there long before you get there. I'll stay away until I see you coming, then will join you in releasing the women. By then most of Phillips's men should be running toward the fighting on the east side of the city. We'll release the women, find Peter's wife and head southwest to skirt the city and head home."

"Then there is nothing else?" Will asked Ulcher.

"We will do what we've been training for. Move in from the east and take out every one of Phillips's men that we encounter. Once we start our attack, we won't stop until we get to the west edge of the city. You'll be long gone by then."

"Wait!" He held his hand in front of him. "Did this Peters tell you where they were building the dirty bombs?"

"He thought they might be in the capitol building

basement. Since he was a captive himself, he wasn't privy to a lot of information. Just what he was able to overhear."

"All right. We'll be careful around every hostage building we approach, but especially careful at the capitol. Good luck." He turned and motion for Jim to follow.

Allison

A soft tapping on her bedroom door dragged Allison from a deep sleep. She reached behind her and felt Bella's warm body snuggled against her butt. Bella's tail slapped the bed.

"Who is it?" Allison croaked.

"Allison, it's me. Jaden. Mary fell down the stairs and Nelda told me to have you turn the generator on so they can bring Mary over here."

"Bring your light in here, honey." Allison's feet hit the floor and she reached to the foot of the bed for her sweat pants. The days were getting warmer, but the nights still gave way to chilly temperatures. Allison saw small misty clouds in her breath.

Jaden held the light while Allison found her slippers. Then, not bothering to remove her nightgown and put on a shirt, she grabbed her own light from the dresser.

"Come on." She hurried down the hall to the basement door, Jaden and Bella on her heels. They moved past the makeshift room where the security detail slept. It was empty now because the shifts were in the middle of changing.

In the far corner of the basement, Allison paused. "Shine the lights here, honey."

Jaden did as she was told and Allison found the switches she needed.

"Hand me my light so I can make sure the breakers we need are on. That will save me a trip down after I flip the generator on outside."

When she was satisfied that all the switches were in the right position, she turned and ran to the stairs.

"Bring your light," she called over her shoulder.

Jaden was forced to run to keep up with Allison. Outside, Allison found the switch that would allow the generator to kick on and supply power to the house.

"Hold my light." She handed it to Jaden and tugged at the lever. It finally moved and the generator chugged as the motor started.

She held out her hand and Jaden gave her back her light.

"Now we need to set the wood panels that will help muffle the sound. Can you start handing me those panels from over there and I'll get them in place?"

Bella wandered between the two of them, her nose

to the ground. She paused before hunching her back. "Not there, Bella," Allison warned.

Bella finished her dump and bounded to Allison, her tail whipping Allison's legs.

"Jaden, watch where you are walking, Bella just left a present right there," Allison called.

When they finished, both were breathing heavy from the workout. They stood in the kitchen listening to the furnace run. Jaden kicked off her boots and stood on the heat register.

"Oh! That feels so good! I remember how I used to like sitting on top of the heat vents at our house in town. My mom used to tell me I was soaking up all the heat and to share it with everyone."

She frowned. "You know, Allison, I still miss my mom so much it hurts, but I don't miss electricity as much as I thought I would. Am I weird?"

"No, honey, you aren't weird." Allison pulled a pan from under the counter and filled it with water from the sink. She set it on the stove and turned the burner on before spinning and hugging Jaden. "It's normal to miss a loved one who is gone. You will always miss her, but one day you will remember only the good things. When you think of her, it will bring a smile to your face. It will make you happy. I promise."

"Do you smile when you think of James?" Jaden murmured.

"Sometimes," Allison said. "I still miss him so much, but I stay so busy all the time that I think my grief just got absorbed in daily life. I enjoy thinking about James. I wouldn't be the person I am if I hadn't loved him as much as I did. But, I know that life goes on without him."

The back door swung open and Nelda held it while Bill Jones carried Mary inside. Mary's husband, Rolly, followed. Behind them were several other members of the community.

"Bring her to the couch," Allison said. "The furnace is on, it's starting to warm up in here. I have water on the stove."

Jaden ran down the hall and brought an armload of towels and washcloths from the closet. She laid the washcloths in an empty pan and poured boiling water over the top.

She pulled several drawers open until she found a set of tongs. Carrying the dry towels in one hand and the pan of washcloths in the other, she returned to the living room.

"Allison, do you have a big tub or something that

we can put the dirty cloths in?" she asked.

Allison felt her lips curve into a smile. "You certainly have learned a lot," she said. "You help Nelda, I'll go get a tub and some Neosporin. That's quite a lot of blood."

"Can I sit up?" Mary croaked.

"I don't know, can you?" Nelda shot back.

"Nothing is broken, if that's what you are asking. I'd like to sit up."

"Let me help you." Nelda put an arm around Mary and gave her a hand.

"That's better," Mary said. "Now, Jaden, I want you to wring out that washcloth and just lightly dab the back of my head. I know I cut it open when I fell."

Nelda frowned. "We've got this, Mary. You just relax."

Mary glared at Nelda. "It's my body. I can tell you what needs to be done."

"And, I worked at the hospital the same time you did. You are good, but you aren't the only one who knows what to do. Now sit down and shut up."

Jaden sighed. "You guys need to stop talking and make sure I'm doing this right because I'm still just learning."

She wrung out the washcloth and murmured, "This is going to hurt just a little, but I'll be as gentle as I can and it'll be over in a minute." She dabbed the back of Mary's head.

Allison started to giggle. "Damn! I love you, Jaden."

"I love you too, Allison. Now, let me work, please."

This time it was Mary who giggled. Nelda joined her.

"It's all yours Doctor Jaden," Nelda said. "I'll just watch."

"Could you hand me those little scissors out of the first aid kit?" Jaden muttered.

Mary jerked her head forward. "You are not cutting my hair off."

"No," Jaden said as she placed her hand on Mary's shoulder and gently pushed her back. "You've got a little piece of skin hanging. I don't think you need stitches, but I want to clip that little piece of skin and I still have to make sure that you don't have any wood slivers from the steps. Please just let me work."

Mary sighed. "I trust you, little one. Do your work."

Jaden finished cleaning the wound and carefully checked the surrounding area for slivers. She looked up at Nelda.

"Before I put Neosporin on it, I want you to take a look and make sure I've got it all."

Nelda gently checked the wound. "It looks great, Jaden. You'll be a doctor before you know it."

"I don't want to be a doctor. I just want to know enough to help."

"Well, you've already reached that goal."

Jaden applied the antibiotic ointment and then leaned back. "Done."

"Okay." Allison leaned in. "Now, Mary, where else do you hurt?"

"I landed on my hip and bounced down a few steps. Nothing's broken, but I'm probably going to have a nice bruise."

"Let's take a look," Nelda said.

"Not here. I'm not pulling my pants down in the middle of the living room."

"Come on." Allison smiled. "Let's go to the

bedroom."

Mary's right hip sported an angry red spot. Mary touched it. "It's pretty painful and the area around it is tender."

"It's a little swollen already too," Nelda noted. "That's going to be a stunning purple tomorrow."

Jaden raised her hand. "The purple color is because of the swelling. That spot isn't getting the oxygen it normally would get so it turns blue and purple. In about five days, it will start turning green and that means that it is starting to heal. It will stay green for a couple of days and then it will look yellow. The yellow will fade away and you'll be completely healed."

She took a breath before continuing. "If it stays red and doesn't start changing color, that means that a hematoma has probably formed. A hematoma has to be drained. There is another reason for it not to start changing color, but I can't remember what it is."

Mary's eyebrows were raised. "Where did you learn all that?" she asked.

"In your medical book that's in the storeroom."

"Well, good job!"

Jaden looked down. "Thank you," she whispered.

"The other reason would be heterotopic ossification," Nelda said. "It's not very common, but it can happen. It's where calcium deposits build up around the site of the injury. They used to do x-rays to determine if that was a problem. If the power isn't restored, we'll have to find another way to determine what we are dealing with."

"So, what's the prognosis, Doctor Jaden? What steps should our patient take to help heal herself?"

"It's called RICE." Jaden closed her eyes and recited. "R is for rest. I is for ice that you use several times a day for 10 or 15 minutes. Never use heat in the first couple days because heat could cause more swelling. C is for compress if it swells. And, E is for elevate." She opened her eyes and looked at Mary. "You will be resting for a few days. I'll do the cooking. We can have a couple of the guys move the recliner to the front of the common room so you can keep an eye on me and not get lonely."

Allison and Nelda giggled again.

"You might as well step down now as supreme leader of our group," Nelda teased. "I think Jaden has the skills and knowledge to do it alone."

Jaden dipped her head and a flush spread across her cheeks. "I'm sorry," she said.

"Don't be sorry," Mary soothed. "It's a compliment. You are one amazing girl."

Jaden smiled. "I do have a question," she said.

"What is it, dear?" Mary asked.

"How come some people say to put a steak on a bruise? Does that help?"

"No, it doesn't help," Mary said. "Many years ago, raw meat might have been used because it is cold, but raw meat does not have any special healing powers and it can introduce dangerous bacteria to your body. If you don't have an ice pack, a bag of frozen vegetables is the best choice."

"Apple cider vinegar has anti-inflammatory and exfoliating properties that can help," Nelda said. "I've used that in the past and it has helped."

"What about herbs?" Jaden looked at Allison. "Can you use herbs to help with bruises?"

"You certainly can," Allison replied. "There is a poultice that I like. You mix Indian Tobacco, slippery elm, comfrey and goldenseal together. Just mix it with a little water and slather it on the bruise. You can wrap plastic over it to keep it in place. Other herbs that can help include witch hazel, cayenne pepper and lavender."

"Do you mix them together?" Jaden asked.

"You could, but I never have. For minor bruises, I like lavender. It helps reduce both the pain and the swelling and helps with calming. Cayenne is a great pain reliever. Witch hazel is what I use for most bruises. Its astringent properties tightens and tones the skin. I like to put a little on a cloth and put it under the ice pack. It helps to keep the area around the bruise drained."

"Do we have witch hazel? Can I make an ice pack and put some witch hazel on it for Mary?"

"We do have a little in the bathroom cabinet. You'll find some cotton balls in a little bag next to it. Go ahead."

Jaden jumped to her feet and hurried down the hall.

Will

The chilly morning air cut through Will's jacket as he navigated the motorcycle toward town causing him to hunch his shoulders. He reached the north side of the golf course and jogged east until he found Peoria Road and turned south.

He saw no sign of life until he crossed the river. Off to the right horses grazed in a pasture. They looked well cared for. About a mile further, he saw a large building that claimed to be an indoor sports complex. Outside this building, he noticed three men. He waved his hand in greeting. They returned the waved, but watched him until he was out of sight. He made a mental note to try to come back and check that building for hostages.

He continued past the fairgrounds observing several more men who ignored his progress. He turned south and cruised through well-kept neighborhoods. He turned left when he reached Edwards Street. At Second Street, he jogged north one block to Jackson. Now he began seeing people. Two men on the corner of Second Street and Jackson watched him, but made no moves. On the next corner, three men watched as he drove past.

He turned south on Fourth Street. The governor's

estate sprawled across the whole city block. Wrought iron fence and brick wall surrounded the mansion. Through the fence, Will spotted a half dozen men, all carrying weapons. They turned to stare at him.

He used his foot to plant the kickstand and swung his leg over the seat, sliding the key to the bike into his right front pocket.

One man broke away from the group and moved toward the fence. His flannel coat was open revealing a pot gut that hung over his jeans. Will met him there, careful to keep his hands where the man could see them.

"What?" the man snapped.

"I need to see President Phillips."

"Not happening. Who the hell are you?" He stepped back and spit on the ground.

"My name is Will Mead. The president will want to see me."

"I doubt that. He don't have time for losers. Where the fuck did you come from anyway?" He narrowed his eyes. "I don't know if I've seen you before. Who do you work for?"

"I work for President Phillips."

"Bullshit. If you worked for him, you'd have a pass."

"I don't have a pass, but if you don't let me tell him about the troops on the way, he's gonna be pissed."

"What troops?"

"President Phillips will want to see me." Will set his jaw and stared at the mansion.

Potbelly turned to the group of men behind him. "Keith, go ask the president if he knows a…"

He turned to Will.

"Will Mead."

Potbelly repeated the name and a skinny young guy turned and hurried to the house.

Potbelly turned back to his group. "Ryan, come over here and search this guy for weapons."

A chunky kid hurried toward them.

Will said, "I have a gun in my holster on my hip."

"Leave it there," Potbelly said, "The kid will get it. Got any more weapons?"

"No."

When the kid reached them, potbelly said. "He's got

a gun in a holster. Get that."

The kid came through the gate and retrieved Will's weapon. He gave a cursory pat down and then stepped back. "He's clean."

"Whoa," Will said.

Potbelly raised his eyebrows. "What?"

"President Phillips is a friend of mine. The pat down I just got isn't good enough. The kid missed the gun in my ankle holster. He needs to do it again."

Potbelly glared at the kid. "Get back there and do it again."

When the kid held up the second gun, Potbelly looked at Will. "Did he get them all?"

"Yep. But if I had been a bad guy, it would have put my friend in a dangerous situation. If I stick around, I'll make sure everyone learns how to do a proper pat down."

Potbelly scowled at Will, then shrugged. "I agree. We do need more training."

Will figured it had taken him about a half hour to get from the farm to the gate. He had about an hour to kill before the shooting started.

The front door to the mansion burst open. A tall, overweight man strode out. He looked like a linebacker for the Chicago Bears. His bright red nose was visible from the gate.

"Will Mead?" the man bellowed. "Is that really you?"

"It's really me."

"Let him in," Phillips called.

Potbelly stepped back to allow Will entrance. Phillips met him halfway and wrapped him in a bear hug. "I wondered what happened to you. Sonofabitch!" He stepped back and waved his hand in front of his bulbous nose. "It smells like you've been sleeping in a barn."

"I have been." Will grinned. "Any port in the storm."

"Come on!" Phillips placed his hand on Will's shoulder and pointed him toward the mansion. "Tell me what you've been up to. No more SWAT team?"

Will moved toward the mansion. "There'll be time for that later. I've got something you need to hear about soldiers coming to take you out. If I understood right, they could be here today."

Phillips stopped abruptly. "Who told you this? My men haven't reported any soldiers heading our way."

"Just north of Peoria. I was staying in a barn. Just minding my own business." He started to move toward the door, hoping Phillips would follow. He did.

"Yesterday afternoon I heard gunfire. That's not unusual, but this gunfire was different and, instead of coming from the highway, it came from the woods behind me."

They were at the door. Phillips opened it and held it for Will.

"After the gunfire stopped," Will said stepping inside, "I went looking. It took me about a half hour, but I found several dead men and one that was still alive. He wasn't gonna last long. He had at least two gut shots and he was bleeding out of several other holes. I started to help him, but I knew he wasn't going to make it."

Phillips listened intently. He pointed to a door halfway down a wide hallway.

They walked into a large office with over stuffed leather furniture. A king-sized desk dominated one end of the room. "Anyway," Will continued. "I asked him who did this. He said 'Phillips's soldiers.'"

Phillips eyes grew large. He shook his head.

Will held up his hand. "When I pushed him to tell me this Phillips full name so I could avenge the ambush, he got upset. He said to tell Phillips that the soldiers were coming."

Phillips shook his head. "Impossible! My men would know. They'd tell me."

"Apparently this guy was trying to tell you. I didn't know it was you at the time. Especially when he said 'President Phillips.' But he managed to tell me that you lived in the mansion in Springfield and used to be a congressman. I figured it out. I came here as fast as I could to help."

"Did you get the man's name?"

Will hesitated. "I think it was Matthews or Matt Hues. He was pretty weak and having trouble talking."

"I've got a George Matthews up north. Kinda short. Bald on top - to his shoulders on the sides."

"Yeah. That sounds like him."

"How many guys were with him? Did anyone make

it out alive?"

"I found six dead guys plus him."

"Three missing," Phillips muttered. "Can you describe the dead?"

"Not really. Anyway, we have more important things to talk about. If that guy was telling the truth, you are about to be attacked. Do you have the men to defend this whole city?"

"I got plenty of men. Hold on." He walked to the door and opened it. "Ziglar!" he screamed.

Pounding footsteps stopped just short of the door. "Sir?"

"Get a team of six. Send each of them to the west edge of town and set up for an attack."

"Who's going to attack?"

"I hope no one, but my friend here says he heard the military was on their way. We need to be on our toes just in case."

Ziglar turned and hurried away. Phillips turned back to Will. "So, what do you think?"

"I don't know what to think. I've been getting by since the solar flare, haven't decided where I want to go or what I want to do. I spent the last couple of weeks outside of Peoria. I knew I didn't want to stay there. I was thinking about heading down to the Shawnee National Forest. If I didn't like that, I thought I'd head to Missouri. When I heard your name yesterday, it kind of brought back memories."

Phillips eyes reddened. "Yeah. I don't know if I ever properly thanked you for that."

"You did."

Phillips walked to a cabinet. He picked up a bottle of brandy and poured two glasses. Handing one to Will, he settled into the brown leather chair at the desk. A map of the city was spread across the desk.

Will moved behind him and leaned over his shoulder. "Show me where your men are. Let's see if we can come up with a plan." He judged the distance to Phillips' neck, noting the man's position in the chair.

Now wasn't the right time. That would come soon enough. The trick was to make sure the mansion was in chaos when he did it. That would ensure he was able to escape.

Allison

Allison collected the dirty washcloths and towels and carried them to the laundry room where she ran cold water in the sink before placing them in to soak.

"Jaden," she called. "Do we have laundry that needs to be done? Since we've got the generator running, we may as well catch up on everything."

"I can collect it and bring it over after I fix breakfast," Jaden called back.

"You don't need to fix breakfast, little one." Rolly moved from the couch where he'd been sitting, holding Mary's hand. "Us men can take care of that just this once. I'd rather you stay here with Mary and keep her company."

He turned to Bill. "You got any idea how to scramble eggs for an army?"

Bill turned from the front window. "I don't mind trying. I wonder if we got any bacon?"

"We're low on bacon," Mary said. "Don said he'd have some for us this week. But there is plenty of sausage."

Rolly looked at Allison. "By now, we must owe

Don thousands of dollars for everything he's supplied us. How are we ever going to repay him?"

Allison smiled. "In labor. Planting season is almost here. After that, the growing season will require extra help and the harvest season won't be far behind. In addition to that, Don wants to build another barn this year. We have the labor he needs."

"But Jensen said that we are getting back to normal. We have gas and diesel now. Electricity could be back in a few weeks. Everything will go back to normal and Don won't need our labor."

"But he has and he will," Allison said. "He never would have gotten his harvest in without us last fall. In January, it was only by our help that he was able to bring those ice blocks from the river. Even if we got electricity back tomorrow, do you think Don could get on the phone and call someone to build him a barn? Where will the material come from? Most businesses have lost everything. It will be years before rebuilding gets off the ground. And, the supply chain is still broken. Even if we can get gas and electricity, that will make things more comfortable but it doesn't bring back all the skilled workers that were lost - most of the things we used to be able to call and order. We'll have to do them ourselves."

"Hmm. I guess you're right. I was just thinking

yesterday about whether I'd open the lumber yard back up after the electricity came back. I wondered if it would be worth it to even try. I doubt my old suppliers will be back in business any time soon."

He turned to Bill. "Let's go fix the army some breakfast."

"I like my eggs over easy," Mary called.

"And you shall have them over easy," Rolly called back. He opened the back door, but stepped back into the kitchen to allow Megan to enter.

"Oh! Hi!" She slid past him into the kitchen. "I was just coming to check on Mary and to see if Allison wanted me to start breakfast."

"Mary's in the living room and Bill and I are going to make breakfast." Rolly touched his finger to his eyebrow in a mock salute. "See you in a little while."

Megan smiled when she saw Mary. "It's great to see you sitting for once instead of running around trying to keep up with everything. It's even greater to see you after what happened. Karen said it was quite a fall. Are you feeling okay?"

"I'm fine." Mary grinned. "It'll take more than a little bump to put me down. How are you doing?"

"I'm fine. It's been a wild few days, but I'll get past it."

"I'm so sorry about your sister and nephews."

"Thank you. Even though I knew in the back of my mind that there was a good chance they were gone, it was still a shock. And, I'll tell you this." She raised her hand and rubbed her chin. "If I ever see that no-good brother-in-law of mine, I will take him down. I will kill him with my bare hands. And that's a promise." Tears filled her eyes.

"Aw, honey, come here." Mary held her arms out and Megan slid onto the couch next to her.

"I don't want to cry," she said.

"Then don't cry." Mary put her arm around Megan and rubbed her back.

"Come on." She patted Megan's hand. "Help me up and let's go to the bunkhouse."

"But doesn't Allison want you to stay here and rest?"

"I'll come back after breakfast. Now help me up."

Megan stood and backed away from the couch. "I'm sorry, Mary. I can't. I know Allison wouldn't like it."

"Oh posh! I do what I want. Now you can either give me a hand or I will do it by myself. I'd rather you gave me a hand."

"Well, crap!" Megan moved to the couch and carefully helped Mary to her feet.

"What is going on there?" Allison demanded from the kitchen.

"Aw shit!" Megan yelled. "Mary said that if I didn't help her, she would help herself. She wants to go to the bunkhouse for breakfast."

"Oh, no you're not." Allison stomped into the living room. "You will sit there and eat your breakfast when it's delivered. I've got a box of DVDs I'm going to bring out and you are to sit there and relax today. After breakfast, I'm going to make a poultice to help with that bruise. So just sit down and relax."

Mary set her jaw. "Allison," she said softly, "it's important in life to choose your battles. I understand how you want to make sure I don't overdo it. But several young ones saw me laying at the bottom of those steps. The fear in their eyes was real. Please think twice before we butt heads."

She took a slow step toward the kitchen. "My hip hurts, but it isn't life threatening. I need to go over there and show those kids that I'm okay. I need to ease their minds. After that, I guarantee that I will happily come back and spend the day watching DVD movies."

Allison frowned. "I'd prefer that you just take it easy. I can let the kids know that you are fine."

"I'd rather let them know myself. They have very active imaginations. Now, I'm done arguing. I've made up my mind. Please respect my decision. As soon as breakfast is over, I'll be back here and will put whatever poultice you bring me on my hip. Now, what kind of DVD movies do you have?"

Allison strode across the living room and opened the cabinet under the television. She pulled out a box and brought it back to the counter. "This is one box. There is another under there if you don't see anything you like."

"I already see one I like. And I want the kids to come back with me and watch it. Can you imagine what a treat we will have? We haven't seen a movie in eight months." She pulled out a DVD and held it in the air. "101 Dalmations. Glenn Close was the best Cruella De Vil. We are going to have a great time!"

She turned and limped to the back door. "Want to give me a hand with these steps?" she asked Megan.

Will

Will leaned over Phillips's shoulder. Phillips had a pen in his hand. He marked the location of his armory and his barracks.

"How many men total do you have in the city right now?" Will asked.

"Three hundred and fifty or so."

"Are there posts around the town or do you keep them moving?"

"I'm not sure," Phillips shrugged. "I pretty much leave that to Paul Richards and George Matthews."

"Was Matthews the guy I found?"

"Yeah, him. Paul Richards runs things when George is out on hunts."

"Hunts?"

"Well…" Phillips reddened. "We send teams out to make sure there aren't any people who need assistance."

"I see." Will picked up the pen that Phillips had set down. "Three hundred and fifty men is a good number. How did you come up with that many so fast? I was sure the guardsmen and reservists would have been long gone. I made a trip to Rockford and there didn't seem to be any law and order left."

Phillips leaned back in the chair, bumping Will. "So, do you think I need to move any of my men to the west side of the city?"

"No, if the soldiers are on their way, I would put fifty or so guys here." He pointed to a mark on the map that was at the far west edge in the center of the city.

"Then, I'd move another fifty here." He pointed at the mansion.

"I'd put at least a hundred at the barracks because it is a central location and we can move them anywhere we want quickly."

"What about the other hundred and fifty?"

"Where are they now?"

"I don't know."

"How did you end up with that many men? Where in the hell did they come from?"

Phillips looked away.

"James? What sort of men am I dealing with? I can't lead if I don't know who I'm leading."

"Most of them came from prisons."

Will arched his eyebrows. "Seriously? And you expect them to die for you?"

"I do. And they will."

Will stared at him for a half minute before he sighed and shook his head. "I sure hope so. Do me a favor and call your head guy in and let him know that I'm the one in charge now."

Phillips rose and strode to the door. "Ziglar!" he screamed.

Footsteps pounded on the floor.

"Stop!" Phillips demanded. "Go get Roberts and send him in here. Hurry up now."

A moment later, Potbelly knocked on the door and stepped inside the large office. Walking the length of the room, he stopped in front of the desk. "You wanted to see me, sir?"

"Yes, I want you to meet Will Mead. Will has been a trusted friend since we were kids. He's been by my side through the worst time of my life and has done more for me than anyone."

He turned to Will. "Will, I'd like you to meet one of my best men. This is Randy Roberts."

Will held out his hand and, after a brief hesitation, Roberts took it, offering a brief shake before turning back to Phillips.

Phillips continued. "Will is going to be the top man here. He will be in charge of training and execution. You will still be in charge of the mansion and my protection detail, and Richards will still be in charge of the troops. But now you will report to Will instead of reporting to me. Whatever Will tells you to do is the same as if it came out of my mouth. Do you understand?"

"Yes, sir." He shot another look at Will. "Some of the men won't like the idea of a new man taking over."

Phillips slammed his hand on the desk. "He's not taking over. I'm in charge. I've known Will longer than I've known any of you and I trust him with my life. You make damn sure that every man out there understands this. And go do it right now. Use the radios. Use runners. We might have soldiers on the way and I want Will in charge. Make sure the men know that he will be taking charge immediately."

Roberts shot a glance at Will. "Sorry. Didn't mean anything by that." He turned and strode out of the room, closing the door behind himself.

Phillips reached into his desk drawer. He pulled out

a radio and turned the knob. "Let's see what those assholes have to say." He set the radio on the table.

"What channels do you guys use?" Will asked.

"This is the only channel we use. Some of these guys aren't smart enough to figure out when to change channels so we just keep it here"

The radio came to life. "This is Roberts. We got a new boss. President Phillips says that everyone will do what the new guy tells them to do."

"Who the hell is he?"

"His name is Will Mead. The president said to tell you that whatever Mead says comes from the president himself."

"But who is he?"

"Not sure. Someone the president knew before. Supposed to be some sort of expert. But he's in charge now and you guys have to do what he says."

"Is he the one who told the president we were going to be attacked because I don't see any sign of an attack."

"Just do it. We've got too sweet of a deal to muck things up now. Make sure everyone knows that a guy named Will Mead is calling all our shots now."

"10-4"

Will leaned back over Phillips's shoulder. He pointed at the armory. "How many men do we have here?"

"Four. Two patrol outside and two inside."

Will moved his finger a couple of blocks to the barracks. "All of our guys sleep here?"

"Except for my personal men. They stay here at the mansion. We will get you a room here too."

"Where are our posts?"

Phillips started on the north side of the city and identified eight posts.

"How many are posted at one time?"

"I think it's usually six or seven. Some patrol and some stay stationary."

"Great," Will said. He slid his left arm around Phillips shoulder and wrapped it around Phillips neck. He used his forearm to squeeze tight on Phillips's Adam's apple, locking it in place with his other arm.

Phillips struggled. He used his massive hands to push back against the desk, but Will was ready. His right foot was braced against the wall behind him preventing Phillips from muscling his way out of the choke.

Will squeezed tighter, applying pressure to the carotid arteries to stop the flow of blood to the brain as well as breath to the lungs. Phillips stopped struggling and his body went soft.

Will maintained the pressure.

After several minutes had passed, he loosened his hold and the body slumped to the desk.

Will slid the map out from under Phillips's head and folded it so that the armory and the barracks were visible. He shoved the map into his back pocket.

Pulling the top drawer out, he found a Diamondback .380 and a Penthouse magazine. He left the magazine and picked up the little handgun. Definitely not his first choice of weapons, but it would be better than nothing.

He bent over Phillips's body one more time. He checked for a pulse and found none. Pushing the chair away from the desk, he shoved the body into the space under the desk. Then he moved the chair to face away from the desk. To anyone looking in the room, it would appear that Phillips had turned away from the desk and walked away. They would have to walk across the length of the room to find his body.

Will was sliding the tiny handgun into his pocket after ensuring it was loaded when he heard the first shots. Picking up the radio Phillips had used, he slid it into his shirt pocket.

It crackled to life. "Where the fuck did those shots come from?" "I think east." "What do you want us to do?"

Will pressed the button. "This is Will Mead. I want every man who is not part of a patrol to meet me at the barracks so I can get a counter attack in action. Get there now. If you are supposed to be moving hostages, leave them in bed. Get your asses to the barracks."

"We aren't supposed to call them hostages," a voice replied.

"Who is this?" Will demanded.

The radio was silent. Will turned it down and slid out the door, closing it softly behind him. He turned right, away from the front door.

When he reached the end of the hall, he opened three doors before he found the one that led to the basement. He descended halfway down the steps, bending to look around the space. Satisfied, he turned and hurried up the steps.

He dashed down the hall to the front door. Stepping into the bright morning sunshine he swung his head left and right until he saw Potbelly.

"Roberts," he bellowed. "Where did those shots come from?"

Roberts stood at the corner of the porch. His back was flat against the brick building. A brick column protected him from the side. "I don't know. I think they came from the east. Wouldn't the soldiers be coming from the west? I don't…"

More gunfire cut off what he had been about to say. He dropped to his knees and peered over the brick wall.

Roberts!" Will stepped toward the man cowering at the end of the porch. "How many men do we have inside these gates?"

"Six."

"I want one at each corner and another one wherever you think he is needed. Preferably on the side the attackers are coming from. You stay here on the porch. Do not let anyone. I repeat, anyone inside. I've put the president in the basement. No one is to go in there until I do. Now, are all the troops at the barracks?"

"They should be. I heard you tell them to get there."

"I'm on my way. Use your radio and tell the men that I'm on my bike and I'll be at the barracks shortly. I don't want any of them shooting a stranger if that stranger is me."

He hurried down the sidewalk, pulling the key to the bike out of his pocket. He started the bike and turned west. Two blocks away, he pulled over and dug through his tank pack. He found the comm unit and quickly attached it.

"This is Will," he said.

There was no answer.

"This is Will," he repeated.

This time Riley replied. "Gotcha."

"Where are you?" Will asked.

"Two blocks east of the building."

"Anything happening?"

"Yeah, about five minutes ago, four guys were heading toward the building. All of a sudden they stopped. Then they turned around and headed north."

"Great. This should be a piece of cake. Any idea

how I can get ahold of our friend from this morning?"

"I got a radio."

"I'll be there in three minutes."

He pulled to a stop behind the truck. Riley exited the driver's door. He hurried to the back of the truck and handed Will the radio.

Will pressed the button. "Will to Ulcher."

"Ulcher here."

"I've sent any man who is not currently on patrol to the barracks at Memorial Medical off Carpenter. You need to break to the north and you'll have three quarters of the men inside those barracks."

"What do you mean, 'you sent them'?"

"I'm their new boss."

"What about Phillips?"

"No longer a problem."

"All right, we'll take care of it."

"Riley and I are on the south side of town. We will be heading out of town by moving south, then west before heading north. When you are coming through town, take out anything you see moving. Don't worry about us. And, hey, I told them to leave the hostages in bed today so any known hostage house should be good."

"Got ya."

"One more thing," Will added. "The armory is on the corner of Grand and McArthur. Four men on duty. Two outside. Two inside. I'd send a team there and take it."

"Will do. Thanks."

Will turned to Riley. "Let's go. You cover my butt."

Riley held back while Will moved toward the church that held the woman they were looking for.

The women were looking out windows when Will approached the church. As one they moved away from the windows. The door was barred from the outside. Will lifted the bar and pulled the door open.

Dozens of eyes blinked in the bright light that filled the doorway.

"I'm looking for Darren Peters's wife," Will said.

No one moved.

"Darren sent me to bring you to him."

A tall woman in a dirty pantsuit stepped forward. "I'm Elsie Peters. Where is Darren?"

"He's north of Peoria. Phillips's men are in jail up there. I'm supposed to take you back to him."

He turned and looked at the rest of the group. "I don't know anything about your husbands, but you all need to leave. FEMA guys are taking the city. Consider yourself liberated. Head south. Out of town. Hide there until the FEMA guys find you. They'll take care of you and help you find your families."

"Come," he told the tall woman.

She followed him out the door and down the street. Upon seeing him exit, Riley turned and ran back to the truck. He had the tailgate open and a 2 X 6 to use as a makeshift ramp when Will got there.

"Get in the truck," Will told the Peters woman. He helped Riley push the bike into the back of the truck and used the green tiedown straps to compress the front shocks and hold the bike in place.

Riley moved to the driver's door and climbed in. Will got in the passenger side.

Gunshots were getting closer. A burst of gunfire in the next block caused Riley to drop the gearshift into drive and hit the gas.

Elsie Peters stared straight ahead, eyes wide – mouth open.

Will turned in his seat. "Excuse me, Elsie. I have to reach across you to get my weapons. I lost both my handguns at the mansion."

He bumped against her as the truck swerved around a corner. More gunshots rang out.

"Whose guys are these?" Riley yelled.

Will tugged at his AR which finally separated from the box that had been pinning it to the back. "I'd guess they were Phillips's guys," he said. He flipped the safety selector switch to the firing position and leaned back in his seat.

"Ulcher said he would tell his men not to shoot at this truck." He scanned the block in front of them.

"Doesn't mean the kids wouldn't just shoot anything that moves."

Will turned and stared at Riley. "Does it really matter who's shooting? One bullet will kill ya just as fast as another. Doesn't matter whose gun it came from. Get us the hell out of here."

Allison

Allison dried the last plate and put it on the shelf in the common room. The room felt strangely quiet without the children studying lessons in the back. They'd been so excited to gather in the living room of the house with Mary and watch a movie.

Jaden and Megan were doing laundry. Bell Wilcox and Nelda Jones had both offered to stay and help with dishes, but Allison shooed them away explaining that some quiet time would do wonders for her.

She filled the watering can and carefully watered the herbs that filled the window. She felt the soft smile form on her lips. Herbs did that to her. Just being in their presence made her feel wonderful.

The door opened with a bang and Jaden entered. Her arms gripped two boxes of folded clothes.

"Hey, Allison," Jaden sang. "You should see the kids over there. They love the movie. Do you believe that none of them had ever seen 101 Dalmatians? The Funderburg twins want to watch it again when it's over but everyone else says that they can watch it another time and they'd vote on a second movie. They're really having fun." She paused and took a breath. "So what are we doing here?"

"I just finished dishes and I was watering herbs." Allison put the watering can on the shelf under the sink.

"Can I make Mary some herbal tea to help with the pain?" Jaden set the boxes on the table. "I think chamomile would be the perfect tea for her. I can put a little honey in it and it will be even better."

Allison turned to Jaden. "We can't give her herbal tea."

"Why not?"

"Remember that we gave her some of the aspirin we have left to work quickly on her pain?"

"Yeah, so?"

"Aspirin can interact with herbs in a way that we don't want. For instance, chamomile could increase her risk of internal bleeding when she has aspirin in her system. In fact, most of our go-to herbs are similar. I wouldn't recommend using any of our favorite herbs with aspirin – except maybe lavender. But lavender is so mild that I don't think it will touch the pain she is feeling."

She reached up and rubbed her index finger on the

lavender growing on the sill, then brought her finger to her nose and breathed it in. "Aww, lavender. So soothing. You know," she said turning back to Jaden. "There's no reason you can't diffuse a little lavender. Why don't you cut off a couple sprigs and take it to the house? Put a pan of water on the stove to simmer and let them simmer. It'll be good for her and the kids."

"Okay. As soon as I put everyone's clothes in their rooms, I'll do that."

"You go ahead," Allison said.

"I'll put the clothes away."

"You don't know whose is whose."

Allison's face fell. "I don't, do I?"

She gazed at Jaden. "You know, you are an amazing young woman. In all honesty, I don't think that I could keep up with everything you do."

She took the three steps between them and wrapped Jaden in a hug. "Thank you for all that you do for us. I'm very proud of you." She kissed the top of Jaden's head. "Let me help you put the clothes away. I'll carry a box."

When Jaden had left, taking a few lavender sprigs with her, Allison wiped the tables and cleaned the chairs around the common room. She moved to the back of the room and tugged the recliner to the front. There was no way she could keep Mary cooped up in the house. It didn't matter if it would help Mary, that stubborn woman didn't like being outside the loop. She needed to be right in the thick of things.

Allison smiled when she thought of how totally opposite she was to Mary. Two completely opposite women, best friends.

She opened the door to the stable and switched on the light. A shiver went up her spine. It had been so long since the lights worked. Of course, the power wasn't on. The generator was powering the lights. But a couple lights on in the barn wouldn't draw too much power from the generator.

She strode to the back of the stable and walked into the tack room. She reached over the metal watering trough they had used several times a week as a bathtub and pulled the horse grooming supply bucket off a shelf.

Turning the switch back off, she went to Showdown's stall. When she entered his stall, he stepped over to her and nuzzled her hair.

A shot of sorrow passed through her. She'd turned chores over to Jaden and Lisa because she'd been so consumed with everything else. Showdown had missed her. She stood next to his face, wrapped her arms around his neck and rubbed.

He nickered and lowered his head. His nose rested on her knee. With his lips, he gently teased her jeans. Tears filled her eyes.

She picked up the curry comb and used small circular motions over his body. She concentrated on his muscles, staying away from his spine and legs. When she glanced at his face, his head was down, eyes closed and his bottom lip quivered.

"It's been a long time, hasn't it, buddy," she whispered. "I'm sorry. I promise I'll make it a part of my routine now. So much has happened this last year. We're going to be okay. We were lucky."

She finished with the curry comb and picked up the hard bristle brush and began flicking the brush on his coat. He closed his eyes and dropped his head. A huge sigh caused his body to tremble.

"Oh, buddy. I'm so sorry. I didn't stop to think that you needed a little routine in your life too. Everybody needs a little loving."

She thought of James and paused. Showdown lifted his head, bent his neck, and tapped the brush with his nose.

She resumed brushing. "James is gone, buddy. I miss him so much. At first, I didn't think I'd be able to go on without him. I didn't want to live a different life than the one I'd always planned for. We were supposed to grow old together."

She paused brushing and Showdown turned his head and nudged her again.

She chuckled and went back to brushing. "I feel better now. I miss him terribly, but I know that he wouldn't want me to be sad. He'd want me to keep doing what I've always done. Helping people that I can help, and sharing my knowledge with those who want it. And maybe someday I'll find another man to love. I'm not searching for one. Trust me on that. But I refuse to let my life be over because he was taken away from me."

She replaced the brush and picked up the hoof pick. He lifted each foot for her to clean his hooves.

When she finished, she stood looking at him. He stepped forward and put his forehead on her chest. She placed her hand on the side of his head and used her thumb to rub the silky fur around his ears.

"I know the girls take you out to the arena for exercise every day, buddy. Do you maybe want to go for a quick ride? No saddle. Just the two of us?"

He nickered.

She lifted his halter from the hook on the stall door and placed it over his head. He lowered his head so she could latch the buckle closed, then led him out of the stall to the arena. He followed her to the mounting block and stood still while she stepped up the three steps and leaned over his back. She swung her right leg over his butt and sat up.

Soft pressure on his left side caused him to move away from the mounting block. She let the rope hang loose and kept her legs still, giving him no direction, letting him choose where to wander. All she wanted was the bond that she felt for this magnificent animal to help heal her broken heart.

Twenty minutes later she slid from his back and stood next to him scratching his ears. "Thank you, buddy."

Picking up his lead rope, she led him back to his stall.

The door to the common room opened just as she was sliding the stall door closed. Jean Schmidt poked her head into the stable. "Where is everyone?"

"In the house watching movies. Want some tea? I was just going to make myself a cup."

"No thanks. I'm just here a little early. Don will be along in a few minutes."

"Do we have something planned?" Allison wrinkled her brow. She couldn't think of anything they had planned.

"Jeff Jensen, the FEMA guy, called Don on the radio and asked him to meet here at noon. He said he has something to share with everyone."

"That's news to me. I'll go round everyone up. We don't have anything on the board for today so anyone not on security duty is off doing whatever. I'll try to gather them up. Could you put a pot of water on the stove?"

Riley

Interstate 72 loomed before them.

"Stay away from the interstate," Will warned.

"What do you mean 'stay away?' We don't have a choice. We have to cross it in order to get out of town. What do you want me to do? Fly?"

"Can you?"

"Shut up. Get your map out and see where we want to go from here."

Will unfolded the map and found the south side of Springfield. "Shit."

"Shit what?"

"This road ends at the interstate. It merges with the interstate and then doesn't exist anymore."

"Want me to turn around?"

"No, I don't see anyone up there and we know there are crazies behind us. Let's get on the interstate and get off at the next exit. We can go south, get away from town and then circle around when we are far enough away."

Riley slowed to merge onto the interstate.

The next exit appeared a half mile away. Riley slowed once again to leave the interstate. He'd just turned south onto a four-lane highway when more shots rang out.

Elsie shrieked and ducked.

"Sorry," Riley offered stepping on the gas. "I'll get us out of here as soon as I can." He pressed his foot to the floor and pressed harder. The truck was going as fast as it was going to go. It began to shimmy. The steering wheel jiggled under Riley's white knuckles.

"Step on it!" Will shouted.

"You want to drive?" Riley yelled back.

"Just get us out of here."

"Almost there." Riley stared at the road in front of him. Another block and they would be out of town.

He glanced to his left. Too late. "Snipers on the roof! Gas station."

Bullets slammed in to the side of the truck. The truck jerked, then surged ahead. Three miles later Riley took his foot off the gas and coasted to a stop.

Will looked over at him, his eyebrows raised in question. Then his mouth dropped.

"Oh shit! You're leaking."

"Yeah," Riley whispered. "Can you put the truck in neutral? I can't seem to get enough energy to move."

Elsie reached up and moved the gearshift lever. Will fingered the door handle and pushed the door open, tumbling to the ground. He rushed around the front of the truck and yanked the driver's door open.

Riley slumped over the steering wheel. His right arm dangled next to his leg, his left arm bent, hand tight against his side.

"Help me out," he whispered.

Will reached inside the truck and slipped his hands under Riley's armpits. He gently pulled him against his own body and slowly lowered both of them to the pavement.

"Elsie," he called. "Please look behind the seat. There's a first-aid kit. Bring it to me."

She exited the truck with a red duffle bag which she sat next to Will and yanked the zipper open.

"Tell me what to do." Her voice quivered. Will watched her hands shake.

"Hand me those scissors," he instructed. He

carefully cut the pants leg from ankle to hip revealing three bullet holes.

He let out a low whistle. "What kind of ammo were they using? It looks like all three of these went all the way through after piercing the door of the truck. Check his other leg for holes."

"How?"

"Cut the pants leg off."

She picked up the scissors and leaned over Riley.

"I can't," she said handing the scissors back to Will.

He yanked the scissors out of her hand and quickly split the pants. Three angry bruises were already forming.

"How in the hell did they not keep going?"

He looked at Elsie again. "Please check the front seat and see if there are any bullets laying there."

She stumbled to the truck and came back holding a dirty napkin in which lay three bullets.

"They're bloody," she said.

"That's a good thing," Will replied. "There should be a green bag in the back of the truck. Please open it and bring me several bottles of water."

"Can't I just bring the whole bag and let you go through it?"

Will raised his head and looked at her. "I guess you can if you can carry sixty pounds."

She opened the tailgate and crawled into the truck bed. When she returned, she had four bottles of water. Will opened the first one and poured it over Riley's leg. He quickly wrapped the wounds with gauze before moving to Riley's side.

He pulled the shirt out of the way and carefully lifted Riley's t-shirt. Gently rolling Riley to the side, he looked for an exit wound but found none.

"Crap! The bullet is still inside. How are you doing, buddy?"

Riley moaned.

"The bleeding isn't too bad, but the bullet is still in there. I'm going to have to clean up the area around it and leave the bullet until we can get you to help. I'll get you wrapped up tight and find some help."

"Take me home," Riley moaned. "Get me to Allison."

Will's eyes widened. "I thought you were scared of the witch."

Elsie sucked in her breath. "You have a witch? Who are you people?"

Will ignored her as he gently worked on Riley. He poured more water on the wound.

"Why are you leaving the bullet in? Shouldn't you take it out?" Elsie questioned.

"I could do more damage trying to take it out. It's safer to leave it until we can get the proper equipment."

He placed a heavy gauze pad on the wound and applied pressure. With his other hand, he rummaged through the first-aid kit until his finger wrapped around a bottle of antibiotics.

"No," Riley said.

"What do you mean 'no'?"

"I mean, just get me in the truck and let's go. How bad am I still bleeding?"

"It's not terribly bad. You have four holes – well seven if you count the exit wounds. None of them look too horrible. If I can get Elsie to apply pressure to your torso wound, you might live."

"Might?"

"It was a joke."

"You do realize that you aren't very funny."

Will sighed. "Yeah, I know. Sorry."

He slid one arm under Riley's knees and the other arm under Riley's shoulders and lifted him.

"Put me down, you big goof," Riley hissed through clenched teeth. "I'm not your wife."

"Praise God," Will said moving around the front of the truck to the passenger door. He slid Riley into the seat, then leaned in and checked the gauze again. A little blood was starting to seep through.

Returning to the first-aid kit, he pulled out two more heavy gauze pads, then closed the kit and placed it behind the seat.

"Let me close the tailgate," he said to Elsie. "Climb on in from the driver's side."

"Just leave me here," she retorted. "I'd feel safer."

Will closed the tailgate and returned to the driver's door. "I can't leave you here. There's a war going on a few miles behind us. Any of those guys who held you might get away. They'll come right through here. You don't want to be here when they do. Anyway, I need you to apply pressure to Riley's torso wound."

Elsie stood looking from the truck to the city a few miles back.

"Get in," said Will.

She climbed into the cab and slid next to Riley. Will handed her the gauze pads. "Put these on top of the one that's there and apply pressure. Keep an eye on the leg wounds to make sure they don't start bleeding bad."

He rummaged through the items on the dashboard. "Hey, Riley. Where's the radio you took from Ulcher's man?"

"Under the seat."

Will reached under the seat, feeling around until he found the radio. Then he put the truck in gear and hit the gas. He thumbed the button on the radio. "Ulcher?"

Ulcher came back with, "Glad to hear from you. Thanks for setting everything up. We've eradicated most of them. A few have slipped past, but I've got teams hunting them down. Where are you?"

"South side. We had a problem. Riley's been shot. Do you have a hospital at the camp?"

"We have a clinic. I'm sure they can remove a bullet and give him antibiotics."

"I have to get around the city…"

Will was cut off by Riley shouting, "Just get to Allison. I'm not staying here one minute longer than I have to. Get me to Allison."

Ulcher came back over the radio. "How bad is he? Can he make it an hour to Peoria? FEMA's got an excellent hospital and staff there."

"Yeah, I don't think he'll die in the next hour. Where is this hospital?"

"Take Interstate 74. As soon as you cross the river, it will be on your right. I'll call ahead and have someone look for your truck coming across the river. They'll take you there."

"Thanks. We'll be there in an hour."

"Hey, Will?" Ulcher asked.

"Yeah?"

"What happened with Phillips? We haven't been able to find him."

"Did you look under the desk in his office?"

"He's awful big to fit under a desk. How'd you get him under there?"

"I just stuffed him. I have to drive now. We can

leave your radio in Peoria if you want."

"Keep it. Thanks again for all your help. I'll make sure it is noted."

"You're welcome. He had to be stopped. Glad we could help."

"You did it all almost single handedly. I got to admit, I'm impressed and we owe you."

Will dropped the radio and pressed the gas pedal to the floor.

Just over an hour later the truck approached the bridge over the Illinois River. Two trucks sat on the far side of the bridge, the drivers standing next to them. Will flashed his lights and both drivers jumped in their vehicles.

They took the first exit and wound around a single lane drive that appeared in the middle of the exit ramp. Will followed. They pulled into a drive marked "Emergency." Three men in white hurried out with a stretcher. They loaded a moaning Riley onto the bed and rushed back through the doors.

Allison

Jensen arrived right at noon. He pulled in to the driveway and opened the back door of his SUV and hauled out a box. Allison met him at the door to the common room and held it open for him.

Setting the box on the front table, he turned to the group. "A lot has happened in a day. I have great news – and a few requests. If we can, let's try to hold off the questions until I've laid everything out because everything connects."

He looked around the room. The faces that stared back at him ranged from distrust to anticipation.

"The first thing I want to share is the great news," he said. "We expect power to be back on in Princeton by late next week."

A collective gasp escaped the members seated at the table.

"Does that mean we'll finally get to watch the evening news?" Nelda asked.

Jensen held up his hand. "Let's wait until the end for questions, okay? Princeton should have power next week, but the outlying areas will not. There is no time frame for when power will be restored out here. They are concentrating on cities and the communities directly in the path between those larger cities. It might be months or years before power is restored to all areas."

"I'm happy to tell you that those of you from Princeton can move back home any time. Your homes will have power. The grocery stores will be open although rationing will remain in effect. That will definitely last months, and most likely, years."

He picked up a paper from the top of his box. Glancing at it, he looked back at the group.

"Schools will be open. We have located some, but not all of the teachers we had before the flare. Of course, we don't have anywhere near the number of students we had a year ago, but we will likely need to replace a few teachers. In the beginning, experience will be sufficient for obtaining a teaching job. I have applications for anyone who is interested in applying for a teaching job."

"Some of you will be able to return to your old jobs, but many will not. We have several options available. New jobs will open up – like the teaching positions I just mentioned – and technical jobs that will help bring things back online.

"In addition to local jobs, I have a list here of government jobs and the requirements. These jobs are not local. The government will relocate you to where they need you."

He looked around the room. "I'm ready for questions."

"So are you saying that we'll get the local news after next week?" Nelda asked.

Laughter filled the room.

"I would imagine we will get a channel or two. It may not be the same programming you are used to, but I bet they'll have a local new channel."

Lisa Grant raised her hand. "Do we have to move back to town?" She looked at Jensen and then turned her head to look at Allison.

Allison opened her mouth to speak, but closed it. She didn't know what to say.

"I guess that would be up to Allison," Jensen said.

Allison shook her head. "I can't believe you would want to sleep in my barn when you can go home to a nice house."

"Well," Lisa said with a snort. "I don't really want to sleep in your barn, but I've fallen in love with every person here. I don't want to lose this family we've created. My kids are respectful and helpful.

Everyone's kids are so different than what we had just a year ago. I don't want to go back to that life. I thought maybe Allison might sell us five acres and let us build a house. Or maybe the neighbor will."

"I like that idea," Bell Wilcox said.

"Me too," Bill Gordon chimed in.

The group turned to look at Allison who sat with a tear sliding down her face.

"I love you guys too," she said. "I can't imagine life without each of you here to share the joys and the struggles. We need to talk about this when we are thinking straight."

Karen raised her hand. "I have a question."

All eyes turned to her. "You say that we are getting power back to Princeton," she began. "I understand that the power won't be restored to rural areas right away, but we've heard that they've had power in the south for a long time. You also say that the grocery stores and gas stations are opening back up but supplies are still limited and have to be rationed. If the power has been on in the south, why can't we just ship in supplies from there?"

Jensen gave her a small smile. "What we've been through here has been tough. Some people, like the people here, have shown amazing strength and resolve. Dealing with the weather and having to do it without power and at the same time protecting each other from bandits has shown all of us how strong we are as people.

"In the south, the power did not stay off. The further north you got, the more damage had been done. But two things caused havoc in the south. First, hordes of people from the north moved south. Some made it there on their own. Some were picked up and moved by FEMA and placed in camps. Many of those placed in camps refused to stay. They left the camps and joined others in their search for food and shelter. Residents were forced to defend their homes from fellow Americans. It was a war zone."

"Now I know that you had bandits here a few times. That was nothing compared to what citizens living in the south had to deal with. There were hundreds of thousands of displaced people fighting to survive, every day and every night. The loss of life in the months after the flare took as many people as the flare events."

He looked around the room and caught Don's eye. "The second thing was what I called Don here for. We need the help of farmers. The flare took down our grid before farmers could bring their crops in. The whole country depends on crops grown in the north. Without those crops, those lucky enough to have power still had no food. While you were struggling with weather and no power, they had power and better weather, but no food. The production of food is top on the list of things the country needs right now. The government is willing to compensate growers very well. We will talk about that in a little bit."

He looked down at a sheet of paper next to his box before looking up. "Factory jobs, clerical job, and direct public sales jobs will not be as prevalent as they were."

"I would think that factory jobs would be in demand," Steve Mattern said.

"Not immediately. There are several reasons for this." Jensen paused and looked at Allison. "I understand that your husband James owned a manufacturing facility in town. What did he make?"

"He made components for major auto manufacturers."

"How many employees did he have?"

"It was around forty or fifty."

"All right. First his facility didn't suffer any damage after the flare. But many, many facilities were damaged by scavengers. They still have to be repaired or replaced. Second, there aren't any major manufacturers ready to start up so there won't be any calls for his products. And last, many of his employees are no longer here. You couldn't just open the doors and start up again."

She shook her head.

"Now, the government is interested in talking to owners of facilities like yours. They could help you with designing new products and training new employees."

"I've got no interest in being a factory owner. I have no idea how to run such a business, anyway," Allison said.

"I could help," David Galen offered as he leaned over toward Allison. "I worked for James for a couple years. I know how to program the machines and would be happy to help."

"I could help as well," Sam Smith said. "Don't throw it away without thinking about it."

"There is another answer if you are interested," Jensen said. "The government could buy the business from you outright. I'm not saying that they would, but if you decide that you don't want to deal with it, I can let them know that there is a good facility right here that is ready to run. Think about it. I won't say anything until you give me an answer. Let's just leave it on the table for now." Jensen reached into the box and brought out a tall stack of papers which he set on the table. He reached in once more and brought out another stack which he set next to the first.

"Alrighty then." He handed the first stack that consisted of a dozen or so smaller stacks stapled together to Bill Jones who was sitting at the front table. "Would you be so kind as to hand these out?"

He picked up the next stack and Mike Grant took them from him and started handing them out.

Don Schafer reached his hand out and silently read the top sheet. His eyes grew wide. "No damn way is this happening."

He flung the papers to the table.

Allison snatched the papers out of Mike's hands and glanced at the first page. Her face fell. "Uncle Sam is your partner." The page showed an image of the familiar Uncle Sam. He held a hoe and was working on a row of vegetables in a growing garden.

Together we will grow food for our great country was the caption under the image.

Allison raised her eyes and looked at Jensen. "I thought we told you were weren't interested in 'partnering' with the government."

Jensen's face did not change expression. He gazed back at her with a calm expression.

"Please just let me go over this and I'll explain my ideas and your options. This is my job. I am required to go over this with you. That doesn't mean that I think you should partner with the government. It simply means that I am required to cover this material with all remaining farmers in this county. So, let's go over the material and then we can talk options."

Allison sat back in her chair and crossed her arms over her chest.

"Speak."

Jensen covered the five-page document very quickly. He explained that the government would supply seeds for the crops they needed. They would provide additional gasoline or diesel to each 'partner.' A government inspector would check on the farm every two weeks and make suggestions and recommendations. In return, the farmer would receive a year's supply of the crop for up to eight people. The remainder of the crop would be distributed by the government at the government's discretion.

"It's still a 'hell no' from me," Don snapped when Jensen had finished.

"I understand and I don't blame you," Jensen said. "Now let me tell you the options the government is offering and then I'll tell you a few ideas I had."

The options were few. A farmer deciding not to participate would not receive seeds. They could not buy seeds from the government and they would have a hard time finding seeds in any store. A farmer who decided not to partner with the government would get a small gas ration equivalent to the same gas ration as a city dweller. He would not be able to purchase extra gas for his farm equipment. The only alternative he had would be to rent his land to the government for a small dividend.

"Still a 'hell no' from me," Don said again.

"All right," Jensen said. "Here's what I think would work. He looked around the room. The government has you by the short hairs in two areas. The first area is seed. Not many farmers would have bought this year's seed last year. The second area is gas and diesel. Something that was said earlier plays right in to my ideas.

"The farm store in town still has seeds. I can't be a party to any deal you make with the owner of the farm store, but I can make sure my back is turned when you make that deal. You can get seeds without the government's help."

"You still need gas and diesel. Because of the inventory system, there is no way that I can allot you more than the share you would get as an average citizen. I can't get you a "partner ration" card if you aren't truly a partner. However." He looked at Karen. "Some of you have expressed an interest in building your own homesteads. We can work with that and get the 'partner ration cards' which Don can use to fuel his equipment."

"I don't need seeds," Don said. "But I could use gas for the equipment. I might be able to plant and harvest with my allotted ration, but it would be by the hair of my teeth. But I won't partner and give up my rights."

"You can have my rations," Karen said. "I love the life we've built out here. As long as I could hitch a ride to town occasionally, I don't need to go galivanting."

"Mine too," said Lisa Grant.

"Mine as well," said Sam Smith. "Well, as long as I'm living here and not working in town."

"No decisions have to be made today." Jensen held up his hand. "I've delivered my news. That's all I was required to do. You guys can do some brainstorming and get back to me in a few days."

"Have you heard anything from Will and Riley?" Don asked.

"I have," Jensen said looking at Don who then looked away.

"Is everything okay?" Don asked.

Megan stood. "Is he okay?"

"They were able to take out Phillips and they made it easy for the commander of the Springfield FEMA camp to take over and rescue the hostages. They did find the wife of Darren Peters. She is waiting for him in Peoria. But there was an incident."

"No!" Megan looked at Allison who had also stood. "Please make Will be okay."

"Is he okay?" She turned to Jensen. "Please tell me Will is not dead."

"Will did an amazing job," Jensen said. "He's fine. Riley's been shot."

Allison felt her heart leap into her throat.

"No!" she whispered before sinking back into her seat.

"He's in the hospital in Peoria. He's going to be fine," Jensen quickly added. "The hospital said that Riley was giving them a shit-ton of grief and demanding to be released so they could get home. They were going to get him cleaned up and remove the bullet and then release him. I would expect them here soon."

"Are we done here?" Allison asked Jensen.

"I've given you the information I was required to give you. I need you guys to talk it over and come up with a decision." He looked at Don who leaned against the wall.

He picked up his now empty box and walked to the door. "I promise I will work with you to find a solution that works for you. And, for the record, I agree with you."

Allison waited until she heard his SUV pull out of the driveway before standing and walking to the room they used for an infirmary.

Allison and Riley

Allison tucked the bottom corners of the clean sheet under the mattress in the infirmary. She unfolded the blanket and spread it over the mattress.

"Do you need any help?" Megan entered the small room carrying a bucket of steaming water.

"Did you put a couple drops of bleach in there?" Allison nodded toward the bucket.

"I did. Just tell me what you want me to wipe down."

"I cleaned this room just a couple days ago. The walls and floors have been disinfected. I also got the bedframes, so really just the tables and anywhere germs might have found a place to live. Get the door handle before you leave."

"Happy to do it." Megan lifted a towel out of the bucket. After she'd wrung it, she began wiping the table.

"Allison?" she asked. "Is there something going on between you and Riley?"

"Heavens no! Why would you even think that?"

"When Jensen said that Riley had been shot, you

went white. Your hands were shaking. I thought you were going to pass out. That's not a normal reaction for you. Do you have feelings toward Riley? I thought you hated him."

"I thought I did too." Allison leaned against the door and stared at the wall. She closed her eyes and took a breath.

"I don't know," she said. "When Jensen said that, I felt the air leave my lungs and I thought my heart was going to come flying out of my mouth. I was terrified."

"But, why? Why would you feel like that if you hated him?"

"I don't hate him," Allison insisted. "He just rubs me the wrong way. He is always in my face. Oh, I don't know." She blew a puff of air causing her bangs to flutter on her forehead.

"He's not always in your face, Allison. He avoids you."

"No he doesn't. Every time I look up, there he is. I guess he's just starting to grow on me."

Allison stared at Megan. She looked around the room, searching for something to change the subject.

"Uhm… how long has this thing between you and Will been going on?"

Megan smiled. "Well, I found out that he was interested in me about a month ago. But, I've been in love with him since day one."

"Are you kidding me?" Allison burst out laughing. "You sure hid it well. Is that why you joined the security team? So you could be closer to Will?"

"Oh, no. I felt like I belonged on the team. Will being the head of it was just a bonus." She giggled. "Got his attention too."

Allison shook her head. "You guys sure hid it well. It surprised all of us when you guys came out."

Megan chuckled. "Small town and all that."

"Megan!" someone called from the common room. "Will's pulling in the driveway."

Allison's face froze in shock. "Oh, my God! I have to get out there!"

She rushed from the infirmary leaving Megan to pick up the bucket of water and carry it out. She followed the crowd out the door to the driveway where Will was opening the passenger door. Steve hurried to help him.

"Get the Sam Hell away from me - you crazy gorilla," Riley snarled. "I'm not an invalid. I can do this myself!"

Will stepped back, pulling Steve with him.

Allison watched, tears in her eyes as Riley slowly turned and attempted to put his foot on the ground.

Biting his lip, he leaned back in the seat.

"Okay. Help me," he muttered.

Will stepped forward and slid his arm under Riley's armpit. He slowly guided Riley until his feet touched the ground. "You okay now?"

"Yeah. Thanks. I can walk by myself."

Riley limped to the barn. As he passed Allison, he winked and said, "Nothing to it."

Allison followed him in and pointed toward the infirmary. "We've got you a bed made up in there. Please go in."

Will caught up with them just as Megan turned the corner. She rushed to Will who caught her in a hug and swung her around.

"It's about time you got home," she breathed.

"Not fast enough for me," he replied. "Anything

happen while we were gone?"

"Well, Mary fell down the stairs. She's in the house with the kids watching movies on the DVD. And Allison... well, we have to talk about Allison."

Will leaned away from her. The question reflected in his eyes. "She okay?"

"I think so, but you aren't going to believe what I think."

"Shhh. She's coming." He stepped away and pulled a handful of papers from his back pocket.

"The doctor said to give these to you. It's a list of what they did and the medicines and antibiotics they gave him in the hospital. They also sent some antibiotics and pain killers for him."

"Why would they want me to know what they gave him?"

"Because they had to practically hold him down to give him anything. He was bound and determined that he just needed to get home to Allison. It was pretty pathetic."

Allison's face turned red but her lips stretched into a shy smile. "Okay, thank you. It is important to know what medications he was given before I do any herbs. Some herbs can react to certain medications. Especially antibiotics. The best thing to do would be to finish up with the medicine the doctors gave him, and once they are out of his system, I can do herbal treatments if he still requires them."

Jaden pushed through the crowd of people standing near the door. "Hi, Will," she said. "Allison, it's almost time to start supper. Mary won't be able to, and I heard that you are busy because Riley got hurt. Do you want me to fix supper?"

Allison nodded. "If you could get Lisa and Karen to help you, it would certainly help out a lot. Thanks."

Allison and Riley

Riley looked much better after he'd eaten a hearty stew cooked by Jaden, sopped up with bread made by Lisa with homemade butter made by Karen.

"So, are you going to give some of your land to the people that want to build out here?" He had listened intently while she relayed the information Jensen had shared and the reaction from the group members.

"I've thought about it. I have always loved my privacy and never wanted close neighbors. Lisa said she wanted to build right across the road from the house but I'm pretty sure I could never get used to walking out the door and seeing neighbors." She closed her eyes. "I think I will offer some of the land on the west side of the barn. I would love to have each and every one of the group as a neighbor, but I don't want to see them every time I walk outside."

Riley chuckled. "I hear exactly what you are saying. I like that plan. I don't see any reason others wouldn't like it as well. How much land will you offer and how will you handle payment?"

"I was thinking five acres each. That would be

enough to have a huge garden and keep a few small animals."

"Perfect. And payment?" His brows rose.

"I don't know. Maybe labor. I haven't worked that out yet." She ran her fingers over the hem of her shirt.

"I can help with whatever you need." Riley looked her in the eyes. "I want to help."

Her mouth went dry. She cleared her throat. "What are your plans? Megan wants to build a house and it looks like Will is probably going to be joining her. That kinda of leaves you out in the cold."

"Does it?" The way he kept looking at her made her squirm in her seat.

"What do you want me to say?" It came out more like a demand than a question.

He leaned back on the pillows Allison had piled behind him. "I want you to say that we are good. I want you to say that you don't hate me anymore and that you won't be shooting daggers at me every time you see me. I want you to say that, if I stay, we can be friends."

She looked down at Bella who slapped her tail on the floor.

"I consider you my friend," she said. "We are good and I apologize for the daggers. I won't deny them. I needed to vent my fears and frustrations on someone. You were that person. I'm sorry. I never really hated you."

She picked up the dirty dishes. "Do you want any more?" she asked.

"No thanks. I'm perfect."

"I'll be back as soon as I put these out on the counter. Uhm, do you need anything? Like to use the restroom or anything. I can have Will come and help."

"First, no thank you. I don't need to use the restroom. And second, if I did, Will would be the last person I'd ask for help. I'm kinda Will'ed out right now."

"Well, you just let me know when you do." She stood. "I'll be right back."

When she returned, she had changed in to sweat pants and an old dark blue sweatshirt with a Chicago bears emblem.

"I'm going to sleep here on the other bed if that's alright. I'll sleep better knowing that someone will be here if you need anything during the night. I've got the pain pills the doctor sent. You'll take one now to help you sleep and just let me know if you need any during the night."

She stood over him, offering the pain pills with one hand and the glass of water with the other.

He stared at her for a minute and then took the pills and tossed them into his mouth.

"I don't snore," Riley grinned. "And I won't need any more pain pills."

Allison flipped the blanket on the second bed and settled in, patting the empty space beside her. Bella jumped up and snuggled in against Allison's legs.

"Well, I do snore," she said. "I'm just hoping those pain pills knock you out enough that you don't hear me."

Allison

Allison rose early. Riley still slept in the bed across from her. He'd lied. He did snore.

She smiled as she slid her shoes on and crept to the door. Bella followed her.

Jaden and Lisa were starting breakfast.

"How's Mary doing?" Allison asked.

"She's doing just fine," came Mary's voice from the front of the room.

Allison turned her head and searched. There, near the front table, was the recliner from the back of the room. Mary was snuggled in, a board lay across the arms of the chair and Mary was drawing on a large sheet of paper.

"Now, if your people weren't so bossy, I'd be standing in front of that stove and breakfast would already be on the table."

"You just take it easy," Lisa said. "You can fix breakfast tomorrow. Let us do it one more day."

"What are you drawing?" Allison asked, walking to

the recliner.

Mary turned the pad of paper so Allison could see. "We were all talking about the houses to be built. I'm going to draw up the plans for a simple twenty-four foot by thirty-six foot two-story house and Steve will help me figure how much lumber we would need for each house. Then Rolly will check to see if he's got enough lumber to do it. We thought that we would wire them for electricity so that when the power comes on out here, we'll be ready."

Allison looked at the plan which showed a simple home with a living room, kitchen and bath on the main floor and three bedrooms and a bath on the upper level.

"I like it," she said. "It looks simple yet comfortable."

She turned to Lisa. "Can I get a cup of coffee?"

Lisa lifted a cup off the shelf and filled it before handing it to Allison.

"Thanks," Allison said with a smile. "I'm just going to take this to the table outside and wait for that beautiful sun to come up over the trees while I do some thinking."

She had just swallowed the last of her coffee when

the door to the bunkhouse opened. She turned to see Riley step out carrying two cups of coffee and a blanket.

He limped to the table and set the cups down before wrapping the blanket around Allison's shoulders.

"I brought you another cup," he said, settling in beside her.

"You shouldn't be up," she said.

"I'm fine. Stop mothering me."

She opened her mouth, then thought better of it and closed it.

"They are really making some plans in there," he said.

"I saw the house plans that Mary was drawing. Looks like they'll be some nice homes."

"Oh, they are done talking about houses." He took a sip of coffee. "Now they are planning on incorporating and trying to come up with rules and a name for the village."

"Oh, Lord." She laughed. "What kind of rules are we going to have to live under."

"Oh, they only want one rule."

"What's that?"

He chuckled and shook his head. "I love this group of people. The one rule they all agree on is 'don't be a dickhead'."

Allison threw back her head and laughed. "They are an amazing group," she agreed. "You know, I've never been a 'people person.' I've never considered myself a 'prepper'. It was my little secret. A secret that I kept even from myself. When this happened, the first thing I realized was that I might be a prepper. The second thing I realized was that I need people. I was incredibly lucky to have found these people.

"Look," she whispered. "The sun is getting ready to come up. I absolutely love watching the sunrise."

He reached out his hand. She looked at it before taking it. When their hands touched, she felt her fingers tingle.

"Do you feel that?" she asked.

"I do."

"I'm not doing it."

"I don't care."

The sun peeked over the horizon. Allison turned her

head. Riley smiled and stroked her cheek. "It's a new dawn," he said.

Thanks so much for reading A New Dawn. (Please leave a review)

While this is the final book in the Allison Series. there is more coming in 'stand-alone' books.

Jaden – coming in late spring 2019. Tells the story from Jaden's point of view. It will include even more information as Jaden learns about herbs and wild crafting. She needs to learn situation awareness and many other skills to keep her safe.

Remember Don and Jean? They were the neighbors who always had goods to share. Jean will have her own story and will finally let you know how Don was always coming up with the goods.

Get the latest updates on the series at:

https://www.facebook.com/ReadAllisonsSecret

Sign up for my monthly newsletter at:

https://www.dlstalter.com

Find some of my favorite Post-Apocalyptic Authors who write about strong women at:

Women of the Apocalypse

https://www.facebook.com/groups/2230796187166759

ABOUT THE AUTHOR

D Stalter is the author of several Middle-Grade and Young Adult books. She lives on a farm in Illinois with a couple horses, a few chickens and the required dogs and cats. She can usually be found in the barn.

She began writing post-apocalyptic fiction in 2018. 'Allison's Secret' is the story of how one farm wife survives the end of her world. The Allison series is considered 'soft apocalyptic'. Not as hard core as many apocalyptic titles, but still packed with action and adventure.

D Stalter

Made in the USA
Columbia, SC
14 July 2023

20485442R00167